More Crummy Teams!
More Zany Players!
More Outrageous Blunders!

Q. What hungry player tried to make a meal out of an umpire?
(See "Down on the Fat Farm")

Q. Why did an American League infielder wear a concession-stand uniform in the 1985 All-Star Game?
(See "Snooze Plays")

Q. What wacky first baseman waved goodbye to ground balls that he easily could have caught?
(See "Holey Mitts!")

Q. What United States president threw out the wildest ceremonial first ball on Opening Day?
(See "Opening Daze")

Books by Bruce Nash and Allan Zullo

THE BASEBALL HALL OF SHAME™: Young Fans' Edition
THE FOOTBALL HALL OF SHAME™: Young Fans' Edition
THE SPORTS HALL OF SHAME™: Young Fans' Edition
THE BASEBALL HALL OF SHAME™ 2: Young Fans' Edition

Available from ARCHWAY Paperbacks

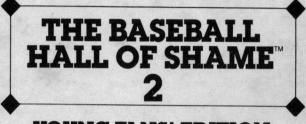

THE BASEBALL HALL OF SHAME™ 2

YOUNG FANS' EDITION

BRUCE NASH AND ALLAN ZULLO

BERNIE WARD, CURATOR

AN ARCHWAY PAPERBACK
Published by POCKET BOOKS
New York   London   Toronto   Sydney   Tokyo   Singapore

AN ARCHWAY PAPERBACK *Original*

An Archway Paperback published by
POCKET BOOKS, a division of Simon & Schuster
1230 Avenue of the Americas, New York, NY 10020

ISBN: 0-671-73533-0

First Archway Paperback printing April 1991

10 9 8 7 6 5 4 3 2 1

THE BASEBALL HALL OF SHAME is a registered
trademark of Nash and Zullo Productions, Inc.

AN ARCHWAY PAPERBACK and colophon are
registered trademarks of Simon & Schuster.

Cover art by Bill Maul

Printed in the U.S.A.

IL 5+

In loving memory of my uncle, Raymond Nash, whose creativity was matched only by his courage.

—*Bruce Nash*

To my daughter Sasha, for whom my love and pride stretches from home plate to the bleachers.

—*Allan Zullo*

ACKNOWLEDGMENTS

We wish to thank all the fans, players, sportswriters, and broadcasters who contributed nominations.

We are especially grateful to those players, past and present, who shared a few laughs with us as they recalled the embarrassing moments that earned them their niches in The Baseball Hall of SHAME.

We want to give special thanks to Donna Dupuy for her fine editing and to Al Kermisch for his outstanding research work. We also appreciate the efforts of Rodney Beck, Phil Bergen, George Castle, Franz Douskey, Tot Holmes, Charles Kagan, and Bill Nicholson. We are grateful for the assistance of Tom Heitz, librarian of the National Baseball Hall of Fame Library, and researcher Bill Deane.

In addition, we would like to thank those who provided us with needed information and material: Art Ahrens; Bill Borst, president of the St. Louis Browns Fan Club; Harrington Crissey, Jr.; Don Doxie; Ron Gabriel, president of the Brooklyn Dodgers Fan Club; Eddie Gold; Larry and Jeff Fritsch of Fritsch Cards in Stevens Point, Wisconsin; Brad Horstman; Mike Imrem; Allen Lewis; Patty McCartney; Ralph Nozaki; Gavin Riley; Joel Rippel; Bobby Risinger; Bill Sabo; Jeff Schector; Rick Westcott; Scott Winslow; and Al Yellon.

Our lineup wouldn't be a winning one without our two greatest stars, Sophie Nash and Kathy Zullo.

Many of today's teams had different names in the 1890s and the early part of this century. In recounting incidents that occurred then, we refer to these teams by their current names instead of the old ones to avoid confusion.

Contents

CONTENTS

WELCOME TO BLOOPERSTOWN!

Soon after our first book, *The Baseball Hall of SHAME,* was published, we realized that a new slate of inductees deserved to be dishonored. Our ongoing research had uncovered many more little-known wacky moments and hilarious happenings that demanded proper discredit. In addition, we had received hundreds of nominations from readers throughout the United States, Canada, and even in Japan. One loyal fan even sent us his picks from Czechoslovakia.

After sifting through all the nominations that were sent to us or found through our own research, we chose those that had the best chance for enshrinement. Then we checked to make sure that these accounts were accurate. We scoured record books, libraries, and newspaper files and held personal interviews. We also had help from the Society for American Baseball Research (of which we are members), who assisted us in verifying the facts about our nominees. The ones that met our unusual standards were then inducted.

What does it mean to be in The Baseball Hall of SHAME? It's a special recognition of a moment we can all relate to—and laugh about—because every one of us, at one time or another, has screwed up.

Former ball player Jimmy Piersall scolded us for *not* including him in our first book. He gave us three reasons why he should have a place in the Hall of SHAME. He once played in a Beatles wig; he climbed the backstop during a game; and he ran the bases backward after hitting his 100th homer. While those moments failed to meet our standards, Jimmy did make it into the Hall for a base-running blunder.

Many former players who had long been forgotten were delighted to hear they had been chosen for induction. At least, they reasoned, they would be remembered for something—even if it was embarrassing but funny.

All of the new Hall of Shamers we spoke with shared a few chuckles with us as they relived their moments of infamy. "Everybody ought to know about what happened," said Frenchy Bordagaray, retelling the story of how he was picked off second while standing on the base. Before Lu Clinton recalled his most embarrassing moment (he actually drop-kicked a home run for the opposing team) he laughed and said, "Oh, God, I had hoped everyone forgot about that."

We give equal recognition to the superstars and the bozos because they all have one thing in common— they all screw up at one time or another. As we say in Blooperstown, fame *and* shame are both part of the game.

OPENING DAZE

The Most Embarrassing Moments
on Opening Day

As everyone knows, the most important day of the year is Opening Day. There is no surer sign of spring. But the season opener is also a red-letter day for those who suffer from a weird type of spring fever that has caused players, fans, and even presidents to make total fools of themselves. For "The Most Embarrassing Moments on Opening Day," The Baseball Hall of SHAME inducts the following:

EBBETS FIELD OPENING CEREMONIES
Brooklyn • April 9, 1913

From the day of its birth, there was little doubt that Ebbets Field would be the scene of some of the daffiest moments in baseball history.

The crowd at Opening Day ceremonies of Charles

Ebbets's new playground was treated to a preview of the Flatbush Follies that would be staged there off and on for nearly half a century.

Thousands of fans started lining up at dawn to get seats. They waited and waited and waited. The reason they waited so long was that the park superintendent forgot the key to the front gate! An official had to go home for a spare while the crowd waited.

Once the gates swung open the fans poured into the ballpark, admiring all the new features. But the builder had left one feature out—there was no press box. The grumbling sportswriters had to cover the big event from the grandstand.

Finally the band struck up a patriotic song, and the VIPs and players started marching to center field for the flag-raising ceremony. But Charles Ebbets broke up the parade when he suddenly fell to his knees behind second base. He had stopped to search in the grass for 15 cents he had dropped. Hot dog king Harry Stevens, who was walking beside him, kindly offered to help Ebbets look for his coins. But Ebbets, a famous penny-pincher, waved him away in alarm, saying, "No, I don't want you to help me. You might find them."

Ebbets caught up with the others just as they reached center field. Bursting with understandable pride, he turned to an aide and said, "The flag, please."

With his face already red, the aide replied, "Sorry, Charlie, we forgot the flag."

FRANKLIN D. ROOSEVELT
President • United States of America
April 16, 1940

One of the duties Franklin D. Roosevelt enjoyed most as president was throwing out the ceremonial first ball on Opening Day.

After eight years as chief executive he had plenty of practice doing the honors. Even so, Roosevelt threw the wildest first ball in major-league history in 1940.

On that fateful April afternoon in Washington, D.C., the president stood up in the well-decorated first row at Griffith Stadium. He was ready to carry on the tradition started 30 years earlier by President William Howard Taft. (On Opening Day, 1910, umpire Billy Evans walked over to the president's box and on the spur of the moment invited Taft to toss out the first ball. Taft gladly accepted.)

Now it was FDR's turn. Like the five presidents before him, he was right-handed. Like the five presidents before him, he didn't have much of a throwing arm. Unlike the five presidents before him, FDR threw a most embarrassing first ball.

As the players from the Washington Senators and Boston Red Sox gathered on the field in front of the president he cocked his arm and threw—and hit photographer Irving Schlossenberg of the *Washington Post* right in the camera!

WASHINGTON PARK FANS
Brooklyn • April 11, 1912

A mob of rowdy fans turned the 1912 Opening Day game between the New York Giants and Brooklyn Dodgers into a farce.

About 25,000 people—7,000 more than could be seated in Brooklyn's Washington Park—showed up for the game. The stands and aisles were jammed because management had oversold tickets. In addition, some fans had sneaked in after breaking a hole in the left-field fence. Once inside, they refused to budge, in spite of efforts by the police, team management, and even the ball players.

The fans stood along the foul lines and ringed the diamond only a few yards from the bases. As a result, 17 routine fly balls fell into the crowd for ground-rule doubles in a travesty won by the Giants 18–3.

When the Dodgers ran onto the field before the game they couldn't practice because the crowd swallowed them up. Park police had to be used to try to push the mob back.

Players from both teams formed a long line and charged the crowd. But the fans refused to move back more than a few feet. The playing field could not be cleared.

Mayor William Gaynor was there to throw out the first ball, but he couldn't see the diamond. Giving up, he just tossed the ball into the crowd. Some fans were so bold they took over the teams' benches, forcing the players to sit on the ground.

The only people who saw the game at all were

those in the top rows, those standing on chairs and benches along the baselines, and the policemen who stood in front of the crowd. After the first inning the cops became so interested in the game that they made no attempt to govern the mob. Two fans who had climbed up the wire backstop yelled down a play-by-play account to the sportswriters, who couldn't see any of the action.

Meanwhile, New York manager John McGraw took full advantage of the ground rule adopted for the day. He ordered his team to loft fly balls into the crowd whenever possible. The Giants racked up 13 cheap ground-rule doubles, while the Dodgers managed only four.

Finally umpire Bill Klem ran out of patience. There was plenty of light left at the end of the sixth inning, but Klem called the game "on account of darkness." It didn't matter. Most fans couldn't see the game anyway.

HOLEY MITTS!

The Most Inept
Fielding Performances

You can tell who they are in the box score by their first initial: E. These are the famous fumblers who make it to the bigs with holes in their gloves. These players catch more flak from fans than balls. They boot so many balls they belong on a soccer field, not a baseball diamond. For "The Most Inept Fielding Performances," The Baseball Hall of SHAME inducts the following:

ZEKE "BANANAS" BONURA
**First Baseman • Chicago–Washington, A.L.;
New York–Chicago, N.L. • 1934–40**

Zeke Bonura was nicknamed "Bananas" for a good reason. He *was* bananas.

Although he was the worst-fielding first baseman of his time, the colorful big lug made very few errors.

Zeke "Bananas" Bonura waved at ground balls.

(George Brace Photo)

That's because he cheerfully waved goodbye to out-field grounders that he could easily have caught. Bonura simply never moved. He drove his managers crazy by giving the high five to bouncing balls that were no more than five feet from him.

After watching Bonura bid bye-bye to yet another easy grounder, Washington Senators owner Calvin Griffith sputtered in anger, "Bonura is a no-account. In more than 50 years in baseball, he's the worst and most overpaid big-league ball player I've ever seen!"

Bonura hit well enough to stay in the majors for seven years, despite fielding that was less than per-fect and more than frightening. Though he went through the motions with lusty zeal and lots of zest, fielding just didn't seem all that important to the 6-foot, 210-pound first baseman.

Bonura was such a laid-back guy that he was al-ways willing to listen to stories from enemy first-base coaches during games. He was being friendly. They were being sneaky. They took his mind off the game on purpose, so it would be easier for a hitter to bounce a batted ball past him.

Every once in a while Bonura lost his temper. When he did, he usually lost track of the game. On April 24, 1938, the Senators were leading the Yankees 3–2 in the eighth inning, but New York had loaded the bases with one out.

On a potential double-play ball the Senators got the runner out at second. But the batter beat the throw to first as the tying run scored. Bonura, playing first base for Washington, whirled around to argue with umpire Johnny Quinn. When he did, he forgot that the ball he held in his glove was still in play. As Bonura ranted and raved, Yankee runner Joe Gordon, who had gone from second to third on the groundout, raced around third and slid across the plate with the winning run.

Bonura turned first base into a shambles when he played for the Chicago White Sox. To make sure that balls hit right at him would not slip by, he used a special feet-together fielding stance that made him look like an overstuffed praying mantis. Whenever he kept a grounder from getting past him he counted it as a great victory.

The patience of Chicago manager Jimmy Dykes finally wore thin by 1937. Especially after Bonura let the ball get by him in a tight game against the Tigers for the game-winning run.

"Could Bonura have gotten the ball?" Dykes asked White Sox catcher Luke Sewell.

"No," answered Sewell.

"Why not?" Dykes asked. "It was hit right at him. What are you trying to do, cover for him?"

Sewell replied, "I merely said Bonura couldn't have gotten it. If you want to ask me about the other first basemen in the league, that's something else."

STAN MUSIAL
Outfielder • St. Louis, N.L. • May 14, 1944

Stan Musial suffered his worst fielding moment ever on a heads-up play.

Stan the Man was playing center field for the St. Louis Cardinals in a game against the visiting Philadelphia Phillies. At age 24 Musial was already a star, both with his glove and with his bat. But on this day he was upstaged by 40-year-old teammate Pepper Martin. It was Martin's last year in the bigs, but the old

"Wild Horse of the Osage" fielded his position like a frisky colt. He dashed back and forth in right field, making one great catch after another.

Because few balls were hit to center during most of the game, Musial didn't have a chance to wow the fans. But in the eighth inning, when the Phillies posed their only threat of the day, Musial finally had the fans buzzing.

With two runners on, Philly batter Jimmy Wasdell lofted a towering fly to center. Musial floated back and waited for the ball to land in his glove. Instead, it landed smack-dab on his head and knocked him down! Poor Stan had lost the ball in the sun.

Pepper Martin retrieved the ball and fired it to the infield, holding Wasdell to a run-scoring single. Then Martin rushed to Musial's side.

"Are you hurt, kid?" Martin asked.

Musial rubbed his throbbing head and mumbled, "No."

"Then you don't mind if I laugh, do you?" Without waiting for an answer Martin doubled over and laughed himself limp, holding up the game until he regained control of himself again. On the very next play Martin made another amazing catch, robbing Tony Lupien of a triple and saving the game.

Martin grabbed the headlines. Musial grabbed the aspirin.

LU CLINTON
Outfielder • Boston, A.L. • Aug. 9, 1960

In his rookie year with the Boston Red Sox outfielder Lu Clinton played one game like a football player and drop-kicked a home run for the Cleveland Indians.

The game was tied 3–3 in the bottom of the fifth inning when Cleveland first baseman Vic Power stepped to the plate with a runner aboard and two out. He slammed a high drive over the head of Clinton in right field. The ball hit the top of the wire fence and bounced back toward Clinton, who was running with his back to the infield.

Before the outfielder could react the ball fell in front of him. But it never touched the ground. The ball hit the foot of Clinton, who was still running, and he accidentally kicked the ball right over the fence! Because the ball never touched the ground, umpire Hal Smith ruled the hit a home run—one that proved to be the game winner.

"Our pitcher that day was Bill Monbouquette," recalled Clinton. "He didn't say a whole lot after the game. He didn't have to. I knew he was really hacked off at me."

AL SELBACH

Outfielder • Washington–Cincinnati–New York, N.L.; Baltimore–Washington–Boston, A.L. • 1894–1906

Fans thought the way Al Selbach played the outfield was a joke. But he was deadly serious the whole time.

More often than not, Selbach looked like a recruit for the Keystone Kops. He showed so much fielding zaniness that his own glove was embarrassed. There was no one quite like him, and the record book proves that. Selbach is the only player in major-league history to own two shameful fielding records—for the most outfield errors both in an inning and in a game.

He first bumbled his way into the record books

Al Selbach set records for the most outfield errors in an inning and in a game.

(National Baseball Library)

when he committed *five* errors in one game as a Baltimore Oriole. He was pretending to be a left fielder in a contest against the St. Louis Browns on August 19, 1902. Three times an easy fly ball fell into his glove, and three times it bounced out and plopped onto the ground. Two times a routine single headed straight toward him, and two times it rolled right between his legs.

Selbach's fielding turned into such a joke that the Baltimore fans made fun of him, jeering and shouting crude advice whenever a ball was hit to left field. There wasn't much else they could do as his bungling handed the opposing Browns an 11–4 victory.

Without meaning to, Selbach brought more belly laughs to the outfield as a member of the Washington Senators in the next year and a half. Having made history as a fumbler in Baltimore, he went after another new record in Washington—and got it.

It happened on June 23, 1904, in the top of the eighth inning in a 2–2 game against the New York Yankees. New York had a runner on first when a single was hit to left field. Selbach scooped up the ball and heaved it so wildly over the third baseman's head that both the hitter and the runner scored. A few batters later Selbach misplayed another single, putting a runner on second and allowing a third runner to score. He was on his way to another record, and perhaps he sensed it. He dropped a routine fly ball, letting in two more runs. All told, Selbach's record-tying three outfield errors in one inning gave the Yankees five unearned runs in the frame. It was enough for a 7–4 New York win.

The Senators were not amused. Just days after Selbach's fielding fiasco, they dumped him.

TOMMY GLAVIANO
Third Baseman • St. Louis, N.L. • May 18, 1950

No infielder ever blew a game more shamefully than Tommy Glaviano.

The St. Louis Cardinals third baseman played the ninth inning against the Brooklyn Dodgers as if he were on the other team.

The Cards held an 8–4 lead going into the final frame at Ebbets Field, but the Dodgers rallied. With one out and a run in, they loaded the bases. Then Brooklyn discovered the secret to victory—hit the ball to Glaviano.

Roy Campanella slapped a grounder to Glaviano, but the third sacker threw wide to second base as he tried for a force-out. The bases remained loaded as another run crossed the plate, making the score 8–6.

The next batter, Eddie Miksis, hit a grounder to Glaviano, too. Once more the infielder threw wide—this time to home—allowing the Dodgers' seventh run to score. Up stepped Pee Wee Reese, who couldn't wait to rap a ball to third. Sure enough, Reese sent a grounder to Glaviano. The ball rolled between his legs as the tying and winning runs crossed the plate.

Glaviano's three consecutive ninth-inning errors gifted Brooklyn with four runs for a shocking 9–8 victory.

For most people, three's a charm. For Tommy Glaviano, three was a curse.

DIAMOND DUPES

Players Who Were Bamboozled
During a Game

Many ball players are con men at heart, making sneaky attempts to trick opponents into messing up plays. The tricksters usually fail because the other players are just as clever as they are. Every once in a while, however, a sucker comes along who swallows the bait—hook, line, and sinker. It's then that the chump who was hoodwinked learns just how far it is to the dugout. For "Players Who Were Bamboozled During a Game," The Baseball Hall of SHAME inducts the following:

JIMMY PIERSALL
Outfielder • Boston, A.L. • Aug. 4, 1953

During his eight years with the Boston Red Sox, Jimmy Piersall liked to be called the "Waterbury Wizard." But he didn't look too wizardly after being taken in by a classic con.

17

In the seventh inning of a game against the visiting St. Louis Browns, Piersall was on second base representing the tying run. Center fielder Johnny Groth caught a fly ball for the second out and threw to shortstop Billy Hunter. With the ball in his hand, the shortstop went out to the mound to talk with pitcher Duane Pillette.

Hunter pretended to give Pillette the ball, but he actually hid it in his glove. As the crafty infielder walked back to his position he quietly told umpire Bill Summers to be ready for a trick play.

Hunter then strolled over to Piersall, who suspected nothing, and struck up a friendly chat with his easy mark. "Hey, Jim, there's dirt all over that bag," said Hunter. "Why don't you kick it and get the dirt off?"

Like a trusting soul, Piersall stepped off the base to give it a boot. Before Jimmy had a chance to move another muscle Hunter had tagged him, and Summers called him out. Red-faced, Piersall didn't say a word. He just glared at the smirking Hunter.

But Piersall got the last laugh moments later. In the top of the eighth Hunter led off with a single and was sacrificed to second. Given the steal sign, he took a big lead—and was promptly picked off.

JOHNNY BENCH
Catcher • Cincinnati, N.L. • Oct. 18, 1972

Johnny Bench, who played in 23 World Series games, was often an October hero. But in the third game of the 1972 series Bench looked more like an April fool.

The Cincinnati Reds star was at bat with runners on second and third, one out, and his team ahead

1–0 in the eighth inning. After Bench ran the count to 3-and-2, Oakland A's manager Dick Williams went to the mound to talk with pitcher Rollie Fingers and catcher Gene Tenace.

It was a crucial moment in the tight game. Bench figured the A's were talking about whether to pitch to him or walk him intentionally. When play resumed he thought he knew what they had decided.

Standing behind and to the right of the plate, Tenace pointed to first base and stuck out his gloved hand. It was the traditional gesture for an intentional base on balls. Bench relaxed and waited for the wide pitch he expected.

As Fingers threw, Tenace suddenly crouched behind the plate. The ball caught the outside corner. Johnny Bench, known as a thinking man's ball player, realized he had been suckered into a called third strike. With his eyes glued to the ground, the embarrassed Bench shuffled back to the dugout, a victim of a baseball con job.

When he was told that Fingers said the pitch was one of the best he had thrown all year, Bench replied, "Why me? He does it when 50 million people are watching."

LEON WAGNER
Outfielder • San Francisco, N.L. • July 1, 1958

If gypsies had known how simple it was to fool Leon Wagner, they would have quit their wandering ways and camped out at his doorstep. He showed what an easy mark he was when he fell for a simple hoax during a game.

Wagner, then a San Francisco Giants rookie, was playing left field against the Chicago Cubs in Wrigley Field. Batter Tony Taylor lashed a first-inning shot over third base. The ball landed fair and then bounded toward the Chicago bull pen, located in foul territory along the left-field line. The hit seemed like nothing more than a typical double.

But then the Cubs in the bullpen led Wagner astray. They leapt off the bench and looked under it as if they were looking for the ball. Their actions convinced Wagner to start a frantic search over, under, and around the bench. But he couldn't find the ball because the flimflammers had given him a bum steer. The ball was resting on a rain gutter 20 feet past the bullpen.

By the time Wagner realized he had been duped, Taylor had already dashed around the bases for an inside-the-park home run.

DOWN ON THE FAT FARM

The Most Disgracefully Out-of-Shape Heavyweights

Much of baseball tradition is written in food stains by players who fight the battle of the bulge—and lose. These porkers handle a knife and fork with more skill than a bat and ball. When they step foot on the diamond there's always the danger it might break beneath their weight and become its own continent. For "The Most Disgracefully Out-of-Shape Heavyweights," The Baseball Hall of SHAME inducts the following:

BOB "FATS" FOTHERGILL
Outfielder • Detroit–Chicago–Boston, A.L.
1922–33

Roly-poly Fats Fothergill looked like a toadstool with a gland problem.

The 5-foot-10, 230-pound outfielder loved to eat. Tigers manager George Moriarty spotted Fothergill

A dieting Fats Fothergill once was so hungry, he bit an umpire on the arm.

(George Brace Photo)

with a big bundle under his arm in the clubhouse one day in 1927. The manager asked Fothergill if he was carrying his laundry. "Laundry, nothing," said Fats. "It's my lunch."

When he reported to spring training in 1928 Fats was so overweight he went on a crash reducing program. He worked out for hours in a rubber suit, took Turkish baths, and followed a strict diet. It was too much for him. He was so weak during the first month of the season he couldn't hit the ball and fell into a horrible batting slump.

He also grew more and more grumpy until he finally cracked in a tight game when umpire Bill Dinneen called him out on a third strike. Fothergill grabbed Dinneen and bit him on the arm. For this shocking action Fats was tossed out of the game. "It's okay by me," Fats muttered to the ump. "That's the first bite of meat I've had in a month."

SHANTY HOGAN
Catcher • Boston–New York, N.L.;
Washington, A.L. • 1925–37

At 6-feet-1 and 260 pounds, Shanty Hogan was known in the bigs as "the biggest catcher in captivity."

He was so fat that when he led off the inning with a walk he filled the bases. He stretched triples into singles.

He didn't run around the bases—he waddled. In a game against the New York Giants in 1935 Hogan chugged toward second base after his Boston Braves teammate Huck Betts hit the ball past the first baseman for what should have been a single. However, right fielder Mel Ott scooped up the ball and threw the lead-footed Hogan out at second.

When he was traded to the Giants, Shanty's awesome appetite gave manager John McGraw a major case of heartburn. McGraw fined Hogan so many times that the catcher cried to reporters, "Mr. McGraw lives in a magnificent mansion, and I paid for every stick of wood in it."

Shanty's weight upset the manager from the very first day the catcher reported to spring training in 1928. After one look at Mr. Whopper, McGraw left orders with the hotel waiters not to let Shanty even look at cakes and pies. But instead of losing weight Shanty added several pounds. An investigation by the Giants revealed a clever plot. Whenever Shanty ordered "spinach," a friendly waiter would bring him half a pie. After McGraw found out, he parked trainer Doc Knowles at Shanty's elbow for every meal. "That guy gets between me and the soup," the rotund catcher moaned.

Before spring training in 1932 Hogan had his picture taken working out on a rowing machine to convince McGraw that he was trying to keep fit. McGraw was very suspicious, though, because the photograph showed Hogan rowing in patent leather shoes.

Early in the 1932 season McGraw told Hogan he couldn't play unless he dropped 30 pounds to a weight of 228. "I can't go hungry," wailed Hogan. "A big man like me can't live on orange juice and a promise." He patted his big belly and added, "This is quite a carcass." It sure was.

CY RIGLER
Umpire • 1906–35

To 6-foot, 240-pound ump Cy Rigler, home plate was something you ate off. He was famous for delaying the start of second games of doubleheaders so he could enjoy a large lunch.

The vendors loved Cy. After the first game he would stroll over to the grandstand and stuff himself, stretching intermission to as long as 40 minutes.

Once, after a game in Cincinnati, the champion eater gobbled down five pigs' knuckles, five orders of sauerkraut, five boiled potatoes, five ears of corn, three Limburger cheese sandwiches, five bottles of beer, and three cups of coffee. Recalled the concessionaire, Hal "Hot Dog" Stevens: "As he was leaving, Cy turned to me and said, 'Hal, thanks for the snack.' "

On another day at Ebbets Field the break between games lasted even longer than usual. The press box gang rigged up a phony telegram that was handed to Cy as he came out for the second game. The wire read: "Hereafter confine yourself to three courses and get the second game started sooner. John A. Heydler, president, National League."

Rigler shoved the telegram into his back pocket and never gave it another thought. He continued to pig out on double helpings during doubleheaders.

JUMBO BROWN
Pitcher • Chicago–Cincinnati–New York, N.L.; New York, A.L. • 1925–41

At 295 pounds, Jumbo Brown was without doubt the heaviest major leaguer to play a regular schedule in

At 295 pounds, Jumbo Brown was the heaviest pitcher in major-league history.

(National Baseball Library)

this century. He was a so-so pitcher who threw fastballs, curveballs, and the biggest shadow in baseball.

The first time he saw Jumbo, New York sportswriter Frank Graham wrote: "He weighs two pounds more than an elephant, but that's an exaggeration—by two pounds, anyway."

The bulk had been standard equipment for Brown ever since the end of the 1927 season, when he had his tonsils removed. His weight ballooned from 197 pounds to a whopping 265 pounds by the time he reported to spring training a few months later. Cleveland Indians general manager Billy Evans didn't want to carry a human blimp on the team, so he shipped Brown to the minors.

Three years later the Yankees invited Brown to their spring training camp. Jumbo had to work out in his undershirt because the team didn't have a uniform big enough to fit him. His weight made headlines on March 3, 1933, when he talked the Yankees into a game of leapfrog. As he leapt over his teammates they collapsed one by one. After the human wreckage had been cleared away, the Yankees were upset to learn that outfielder Sam Byrd and catcher Cy Perkins had been injured.

Even so, the Yankees kept Jumbo on their roster and billed him as "the man who swallowed a taxicab." Of course, pitching during the dog days of summer was rough for such a fat player. In a game on June 10, 1933, he took himself out because he was too tired and woozy—"which was just as well for all concerned," read a newspaper account of the game. "For one thing, carrying him out would have taxed the strength of all the other Yankees put together."

SNOOZE PLAYS

The Most Mind-Boggling
Mental Miscues

*Major leaguers pay close attention to every pitch,
every batted ball, every play, right? Baloney!
These guys get lost in their thoughts and day-
dream just like any working stiff. The only difference is that their office is the playing field.
When they get caught napping, they're in for a
rude awakening. For "The Most Mind-Boggling
Mental Miscues," The Baseball Hall of SHAME
inducts the following:*

CLEVELAND INDIANS
July 25, 1983

No wonder the Cleveland Indians finished last in the
American League East. They not only couldn't win,
they showed thousands of fans they couldn't count
either.

They looked like preschool dropouts when the entire team ran off the field with only two outs—in the middle of an inning.

It happened in the bottom of the sixth inning in a game against the Kansas City Royals. Cleveland pitcher Neal Heaton had walked Hal McRae to start the frame and coaxed Amos Otis into grounding into a double play.

Then, to everyone's surprise, Heaton walked toward the dugout, followed by the rest of the Indians, as if there were three outs. From the dugout, Indians manager Mike Ferraro and the other players shouted at the team to stay on the field.

But the Tribe paid as much attention to them as they did to the scoreboard. Once they realized their folly the players sheepishly returned to the field and eventually lost, 6–1.

"How are you supposed to win a game when you don't know how many outs there are?" fumed Ferraro. "It's one thing to lose, it's another to look bad while doing it. I don't know where these guys have their heads, but it's not in the game."

PEE WEE REESE
Shortstop • Brooklyn • July 12, 1947

Pee Wee Reese found to his never-ending embarrassment that common courtesy has no business on the ball diamond.

In the bottom of the third inning of a home game against the Chicago Cubs the Dodger shortstop was taking a lead off first base when batter Dixie Walker

Pee Wee Reese discovered the hard way that nice guys finish last.

(UPI/Bettmann Newsphotos)

swung with all his might and missed. The bat slipped out of Walker's hands and sailed toward first base.

Being the nice guy that he was, Reese ambled off the bag to pick up the bat. But he left his brains behind. As the "Little Colonel" stooped down to get the bat, Cubs catcher Clyde McCullough fired the ball to first baseman Eddie Waitkus, who tagged Reese out.

Reese should have known better. After all, he played for years under manager Leo Durocher, who always said, "Nice guys finish last."

DICK BARTELL
Shortstop • Detroit, A.L. • Oct. 8, 1940

They called it "The $50,000 Snooze."

Shortstop Dick Bartell, known for his heads-up play, was caught with his head down at a crucial moment in the seventh and deciding game in the 1940 World Series.

His shocking mental mistake cost the Detroit Tigers the world championship—and $50,000, the difference between their share of the winnings and that of the victorious Cincinnati Reds.

The Tigers were winning 1–0 in the bottom of the seventh inning when Cincinnati's Frank McCormick doubled. The next batter, Jimmy Ripple, followed with another double. But McCormick, thinking the ball might be caught, held up for a few seconds. When the ball hit the wall he started for third, slowed almost to a walk after rounding the bag, then took off for home.

Any other time, McCormick would have been thrown

out by 20 feet. But Bartell had his back turned as he caught the throw from right fielder Bruce Campbell. The little shortstop never bothered to turn around as McCormick headed toward the plate. The alarmed Tiger infield yelled like mad and waved their arms to wake Bartell up, but he stood still, calmly turning the ball over and over in his paws.

While he did, McCormick crossed the plate standing up for the tying run. Moments later Ripple scored the winning run.

"I thought, of course, that McCormick was home long before I got the ball from Campbell, and all I was thinking about was holding Ripple on second," Bartell said. "But I must have looked bad."

He sure did.

LOU WHITAKER
Second Baseman • Detroit, A.L. • July 16, 1985

Fans chose Lou Whitaker to start at second base in the 1985 All-Star Game for his glove and stick. He sure wasn't chosen for his memory.

Whitaker arrived at the Minneapolis Metrodome ready to play, but with nothing to wear. In one of the most embarrassing mental blunders in the history of the midseason classic, the American League All-Star forgot to bring his uniform and gear. He left it all in the backseat of his Mercedes-Benz at home in Bloomfield Hills, Michigan.

An emergency effort to get another uniform flown in from Detroit failed when it was lost in transit. As a result, Whitaker was forced to dress up like a Little Leaguer.

He bought a Tigers jersey and cap from a Metrodome concession stand for $15 and had a number 1 written in blue felt-tip pen on the back. He borrowed a pair of pants, and the Twins lent him a pair of the team's blue socks.

The Mizuno company, which paid Whitaker $5,000 a year to wear its shoes, was on hand to present him with a pair of white shoes for the occasion. Finally he borrowed a glove from Baltimore shortstop Cal Ripken, Jr. But Whitaker had to tape over the brand name because a rival company paid him $9,000 a year to wear *its* glove.

BABE HERMAN
Outfielder • Cincinnati, A.L. • April 26, 1932

When the game was over, Babe Herman's teammates left the day's trials and triumphs behind them at the ballpark. But not Herman. What he left behind was his little boy.

Herman didn't mean to do it. He just plain forgot his seven-year-old son Bobby.

About six weeks after he had been traded to the Cincinnati Reds by the Brooklyn Dodgers, Herman was baby-sitting for Bobby. His wife had stayed behind in Brooklyn to take care of their two-year-old son, Donny, who was ill.

On April 26 Herman took Bobby with him to Crosley Field and told the boy to wait for him by the back of the stands after the game. Herman played great that day. Afterward he happily showered, shaved, and dressed. Then, still on cloud nine, Herman hitched a ride home with his manager, Dan Howley.

Babe Herman was so forgetful that he once left his 7-year-old son behind at the ballpark.

(George Brace Photo)

Meanwhile, being a good little boy, Bobby did as he was told and stood outside the ballpark waiting for his no-show father.

When Herman was almost home, Howley turned to him and said, "Geez, we left the kid!" Herman made a fast phone call to the park and learned to his relief that the team secretary had found Bobby and was bringing him home.

Recalled Herman with a chuckle, "I guess I had too much on my mind that day."

HITLESS WONDERS

The Most Inglorious Appearances
at the Plate

Every team is saddled with terrible hitters, guys who call it a good day if they go 1 for 5. They hit for averages that aren't even good for bowling. Why, these players couldn't hit the floor if they fell out of bed. They would strike out trying to hit the ball off a T-ball stand. For "The Most Inglorious Appearances at the Plate," The Baseball Hall of SHAME inducts the following:

RAY OYLER
Shortstop • Detroit–Seattle–Cleveland, A.L.
1965–70

Ray Oyler was born an easy out. He lived in a slump his entire major league career, becoming the pitcher's best friend.

The shortstop, whose weak stick accounted for an

appalling .175 lifetime average, batted only .135 in 1968. It was the lowest one-season mark ever for a major leaguer who has seen action in 100 or more games.

He was an outstanding fielder, but the fans in Detroit didn't seem to care about that. On Opening Day in 1968 they booed him as he ran onto the field with the starting lineup at Tiger Stadium.

Tiger fans never treated Oyler the way the Seattle Pilots fans did the following year. When he stepped to the plate for his first at-bat in a Seattle uniform, horns blew, confetti flew, and signs fluttered. The first meeting of the Ray Oyler Fan Club had come to order.

Oyler's fan club was the brainchild of KVI radio disc jockey Bob Hardwick. He was looking over the list of players for whom the Pilots had paid $175,000 each in the American League expansion draft. Oyler's .135 batting average really caught the deejay's eye.

This wasn't much bang for the buck, Hardwick figured, and it was obvious Oyler would need help. So the Ray Oyler Fan Club was formed. By the first month of the season, more than 5,000 members had joined. The only requirement was a horn, enthusiasm, and "an abiding faith in the power of positive thinking."

Their joy turned to rage when their hero was decked in a fight against Kansas City's Jim Campanis on April 22, 1969. Fan club president Hardwick sent an angry telegram to Royals general manager Cedric Tallis that said, in part, "Five thousand members of the Ray Oyler Fan Club protest the slugging of our beloved leader. Please do not misinterpret our club motto, 'Sock it to Ray Oyler,' as this is an expression of encouragement."

The loyalty of the Seattle fans inspired the 165-pound shortstop. That year he hit his weight, literally.

JOHNNY BROACA
Pitcher • New York–Cleveland, A.L. • 1934–39

To Johnny Broaca, batting was like an algebra class—he didn't want to go, but he had no choice.

Broaca simply hated to bat.

"I've never seen anything like it," said former batting star George Kell. "No player ever would pass up a chance to hit morning, noon, or night—not even if he couldn't hit his hat size."

Broaca would indeed pass up the chance. Even on the days he was scheduled to pitch, Broaca holed up in the clubhouse rather than go out and take his licks in the batting cage.

This amazing allergy to hitting showed up in Broaca's batting average. During his six years in the bigs he made 254 trips to the plate and somehow collected 23 hits. He left the game with a lousy lifetime average of .091.

His first hit was really an accident. In a game against the Senators on July 1, 1934, Broaca took his usual stance at the plate, his bat planted firmly on his shoulder. The pitch sailed high and inside and glanced off the bat that still rested on Broaca's shoulder. To everyone's shock—most of all Broaca's—the ball bounced over third base for a hit.

A week earlier Broaca had etched his name in the record books. Thanks to his severe batting allergy, Broaca broke out with a record-tying rash of strikeouts batting against the White Sox on June 25. Five times he trudged up to the plate. Five times he retreated to the safety of the dugout after striking out.

He was a little premature on one strikeout, though. While doing his imitation of a statue in the batter's box, Broaca ran the count to 2-and-2. Before the next

Johnny Broaca simply hated to bat.

(George Brace Photo)

pitch was called by umpire George Moriarty, Broaca—
hoping and praying it was strike three—turned away,
marched back to the dugout, and sat down.

Puzzled, Moriarty wandered over. "I'm sorry,
Johnny," the ump said. "That was ball three. You'll
have to come back."

HANK AGUIRRE
Pitcher • Cleveland–Detroit, A.L.;
Los Angeles–Chicago, N.L. • 1955–70

All pitchers have a license to be lousy hitters, but
Hank Aguirre should have had his taken away.

In nine of his 16 seasons in the bigs he batted under
.100, and he went hitless in five of those years. In 388
at-bats he struck out 68 percent of the time, and he collected only 33 hits for an awful lifetime average of .085.

Aguirre was so pitiful at the plate that when he
finally got his first hit after going 0 for 2 years, the
fans gave him a standing ovation.

It happened in his eighth season. The Detroit Tigers had tried everything they could think of to put
some muscle in his weak swing. He took extra batting
practice, followed special coaching instructions, and
studied films of himself. He even accepted a coach's
offer of a free steak dinner if he'd get a hit.

One thing Aguirre hadn't tried was batting left-
handed. In a game against the Yankees at Tiger Stadium
on June 22, 1962, Aguirre swatted from the southpaw
side of the plate for the first time in his life. Lo and
behold, he hit a soft drive that fell into short right field
for an RBI single! The 43,723 fans went wild. They
stood and cheered for a full five minutes in the kind of
ovation that even Mickey Mantle had never heard.

"My gosh, I've been batting the wrong way my entire life!" declared Aguirre, whose batting average soared from .000 to an awesome .009.

Actually, Aguirre did get a hit the week before. He smacked a tennis ball to left field for a double in a father-son game.

After the Yankee game sportswriters crowded around Aguirre. "I figured I'd win the MHH award for most horrible hitting," he said. "Now maybe they'll let me order some bats with my own name on them."

It didn't matter what bat he used or which side of the plate he swung from. He collected only one more hit the rest of the year. "I think my hitting is progressing," he said at the time. "It's becoming progressively worse."

He did enjoy one great moment on June 4, 1967, and once again it was against the Yankees. Pitcher Fritz Peterson had intentionally walked Ray Oyler, a .186 hitter, to load the bases and get at Hammerless Hank. Aguirre took two quick strikes and then somehow managed to slam the first triple of his life.

After sliding into third base the excited Aguirre whispered to coach Tony Cuccinello, "I'm gonna steal home." The coach shook his head and said, "Hank, it took you 13 years to get here, so don't fool around."

RON HERBEL
Pitcher • San Francisco–San Diego–New York–Atlanta, N.L. • 1963–71

Ron Herbel deserved to be poster child for the designated hitter rule.

The right-handed pitcher with the thick eyeglasses

had no business touching a bat, let alone swinging one. He holds the record for the lowest career batting average of anyone who has batted at least 100 times—a nearly invisible .029. Herbel went hitless in five seasons, topped by an 0 for 47 mark in 1964 that ranks as the third worst single year in major league history.

After 56 attempts Herbel banged out his first hit in the Astrodome on May 21, 1965. It gave him an excuse to explain his batting technique to reporters. "In the minors," he said, "once in a while I'd close my eyes and get a hit. The pitcher would usually have to hit my bat, though."

Herbel would have collected his second hit in Wrigley Field on September 4, 1965, if he had known what to do. But he was so surprised at rapping a clean shot to right field that he forgot to run fast enough. Cubs right fielder Billy Williams threw him out at first base.

Instead, he got his next hit the following year, in the Astrodome. When he did, the Giants publicity department decided to promote his hitting, or rather the lack of it. In the 1967 media guide they added a footnote to Herbel's statistics. It pointed out that his only two hits in 134 at-bats had been indoors. "I've never heard of a pitcher's batting record included in a club's press guide," Herbel grumbled. "Somebody really knows how to hurt a guy."

On April 16, 1967, Herbel finally got his first outdoor hit—a ground-rule double, no less. That's the good news.

The bad news is that he got picked off second on the very next play.

Run for Your Lives!

The Most Outrageous
Base-Running Blunders

Some players are such rotten runners they could use a second-base coach. It's not that their legs are slow; it's that their minds never get out of first gear. To others, running the base paths seems as foolish as strolling down a dark alley at midnight. For "The Most Outrageous Base-Running Blunders," The Baseball Hall of SHAME inducts the following:

DAN FORD
Outfielder • Minnesota, A.L. • Sept. 5, 1978

Minnesota Twins manager Gene Mauch paced his office, fuming, and declared, "All I've got to say is that the man will not get paid for tonight's game."

His anger was aimed at Twins center fielder Dan Ford, for the dumbest base-running blunder that the veteran manager—and most baseball observers—had ever seen.

Minnesota was losing to the visiting Chicago White Sox 4–0 in the bottom of the seventh inning when the Twins loaded the bases with Ford on third, Jose Morales on second, and Larry Wolfe on first. When Bombo Rivera lined a one-out single to center, Ford backpedaled down the third-base line, waving his arms and yelling, "C'mon, Jose! C'mon, Jose!" to Morales, who was trying to score from second.

What was wrong with Ford's rah-rah was that he had stopped short of home plate and was cheering for his teammate, who flew past him and touched home. Ford suddenly realized that *he* hadn't crossed the plate, and he quickly touched it with his toe. But White Sox catcher Bill Nahorodny noticed the mixup and shouted at umpire Joe Brinkman, who called Morales out for passing Ford.

Mauch ran out of the dugout and, with a defeated look on his face, asked Brinkman, "Did what I think happened, happen?" The ump nodded. Mauch turned away without protest. As he headed back to the dugout with the downcast and embarrassed Ford, Mauch growled, "Just keep right on going." Ford went right into the clubhouse and left the stadium before the end of the game.

Instead of two runs and one out, the Twins had one run and two outs. The play took on added meaning because Minnesota lost 4–3.

That wasn't the only time Ford blundered badly on the base paths that year. In a game against the Detroit Tigers, Ford was motoring from first to third on a single. The throw from the outfield was way off, forcing third baseman Aurelio Rodriguez to scamper 15 feet from the base to make the catch.

Ford would have made it safely to third—if only he had slid into the base, instead of into Rodriguez.

OLLIE O'MARA
Shortstop • Brooklyn, N.L. • 1916

Somewhere between home plate and first base Ollie O'Mara lost his mind.

In a game against the New York Giants, the Brooklyn Dodgers had Hy Myers on first base and Jack Coombs on second. O'Mara stepped up to the plate with orders to bunt and dropped a slow roller along the third-base line. Catcher Bill Rariden grabbed the ball but threw wildly to third, trying to catch Coombs coming from second. Almost at the same moment Rariden yelled, "Foul ball!" He hoped to wipe out his error by tricking umpire Bill Klem into thinking the ball wasn't fair.

O'Mara had started for first but turned around and headed back toward the batter's box after he heard someone shout that it was a foul.

But Klem yelled, "Fair ball!"

Unaware of the wild throw, O'Mara bellowed back, "Foul ball!"

Klem insisted otherwise and thundered, "Fair ball!"

Meanwhile, left fielder George Burns was chasing the ball, which by now had rolled all the way to the fence. As O'Mara argued with the umpire, four Dodgers jumped out of the dugout, raced up, and urged him to start running. But the hardheaded O'Mara refused to listen and remained at the plate.

After hitting the ball, Ollie O'Mara once had to be dragged down to first base by his teammates.

(George Brace Photo)

While the debate raged, base runners Coombs and Myers scored, and Burns tracked down the ball. Finally, the Brooklyn strong-arm squad grabbed O'Mara and hustled him down the first-base line, kicking, punching, and screaming at his teammates.

It was all for nothing, though. O'Mara—and his escorts—were thrown out at first base by ten feet.

WILLIE STARGELL
First Baseman • Pittsburgh, N.L.
Sept. 19, 1978

Willie Stargell couldn't believe his eyes. Pittsburgh Pirates manager Chuck Tanner had given him the steal sign.

Stargell, whose legs could hardly shift from neutral to first gear, stole bases about as often as an eclipse of the sun. But on this particular day, with the Pirates romping over the Chicago Cubs at Wrigley Field, he thought, "Who am I to argue with Tanner?"

So Stargell lumbered toward second in one of the silliest base-stealing attempts ever seen in the majors.

The paunchy 38-year-old veteran ran as fast as he could, but even his own shadow had passed him. When Stargell was about two thirds of the way to second he began a slide that made him look more like a beached whale than a ball player.

He came to a dead stop about ten feet from the bag. Closing in on the reclining runner, Cubs shortstop Ivan DeJesus was about to make an easy tag. But Stargell's mind was quicker than his legs, and he decided there was one possible way out of his predicament. He stood up, formed a *T* with his hands, and shouted, "Time out!" The only "out" the umpire called was Stargell, who returned to a dugout that was rocking with laughter. After one teammate caught his breath, he asked Stargell why he slid so soon.

"I was given some bad information," Stargell answered with a straight face. "I was told the bases were only 80 feet apart."

GARY GEIGER
Outfielder • Boston, A.L. • June 8, 1961

Gary Geiger went from hero to zero in a matter of seconds when he hit what he thought was a game-winning triple. Unfortunately, it wasn't.

In a long night game against the visiting Los Angeles Angels, the Boston Red Sox entered the bottom of the eleventh inning losing 4–3. But leadoff hitter Chuck Schilling walked, and Geiger smashed a pitch off the center-field wall to drive Schilling home.

As Geiger pulled into third his teammates cheered. Now they were in a 4–4 tie with a runner on third and no one out. Suddenly, to their shocked amazement, Geiger was trotting joyfully past third as if he were waiting for their congratulations.

The chowderhead had forgotten the score! He hadn't realized that his hit had only tied the game—it didn't win it. Geiger quickly came to his senses when he was tagged out in a base-running blunder that ultimately cost his team a victory.

"I thought the score was tied when I hit the ball," the downcast outfielder confessed after the game. "When I ran to third I saw Schilling score. I thought the winning run was in. Then I heard [third-base

coach] Billy Herman yelling at me, and I turned back.
I thought I was going to be congratulated for having
knocked in the run. But then I got caught in a run-
down, and that was it.''

The next batter, Carl Yastrzemski, hit what would
have been a game-winning sacrifice fly—if it hadn't
been for Geiger's boo-boo. The game ended in a tie in
the twelfth inning because of a downpour. The entire
game had to be replayed the next day as part of a
doubleheader. The Angels won the makeup game 5–1,
much to the dismay of Gary Geiger.

BOBBY MEACHAM   DALE BERRA
Shortstop   Third Baseman
New York, A.L. • Aug. 2, 1985

LOU GEHRIG   DIXIE WALKER
First Baseman   Outfielder
New York, A.L. • April 29, 1933

The Baseball Hall of SHAME would be remiss if it
did not pay special dishonor to four New York Yankees who proved that history—no matter how un-
believable—does repeat itself.

In the wildest base-running fiasco ever witnessed at
Yankee Stadium, Bobby Meacham and Dale Berra
were tagged out in wham-bam order at home plate on
the same play. What made it so incredible was that
the rare base-path blunder was not the first of its kind
committed by the Yankees. Fifty-two years earlier,
stars Lou Gehrig and Dixie Walker ran into the same
double trouble at home plate in almost exactly the
same botched-up way.

In both cases the boneheaded play cost the Yankees a chance at victory. The difference was that the old-time pinstripers embarrassed themselves before just 36,000 fans. Berra and Meacham made fools of themselves on national television in front of millions.

In the modern version, Meacham was on second base and Berra on first in the seventh inning of a 3–3 tie with the visiting Chicago White Sox. Teammate Rickey Henderson smacked a booming drive to left-center field, which should have been a two-run double. But Henderson's mighty blow turned into a 400-foot, double-play single.

Meacham, waiting to see if the ball would be caught, held at second. Berra, believing it would fall, took off from first. As the ball hit the ground Meacham stumbled and then headed for third with Berra right on his heels.

When they reached third, coach Gene Michael waved Meacham—but not Berra—home. Berra must have figured that what was good enough for Meacham was good enough for him. He also sprinted around third, causing Michael to throw his arms in the air in confusion. Waiting at the plate was catcher Carlton Fisk, who caught a perfect relay throw. Fisk tagged out Meacham in a collision and then spun around to tag Berra. It was your typical 8-to-6-to-2-to-2 double play.

New York manager Billy Martin was so upset at Berra that he benched him on the spot. The startling double play ruined a Yankee scoring threat, and the team lost 6–5 in 11 innings. Fumed Martin, "I've never seen a play like that in grammar school, let alone the major leagues."

That's because Martin wasn't even five years old

Runners Bobby Meacham and Dale Berra were tagged out at home plate—on the same play.

(New York Daily News Photo)

when Lou Gehrig and Dixie Walker pulled the same base-running boner back in 1933.

In that game the Yankees were losing to the Washington Senators 6–3 in the bottom of the ninth. With Gehrig on second base and Walker on first, Tony Lazzeri walloped a shot to right-center field. Like Rickey Henderson's drive, Lazzeri's potential two-run double turned into a shocking 400-foot, double-play single.

Thinking the ball might be caught, Gehrig cautiously hugged second while Walker, head down, sprinted from first. When the ball fell safely Gehrig took off and rounded third only a few feet ahead of Walker. The two looked like relay runners ready to exchange the baton as they dashed for home.

Meanwhile, catcher Luke Sewell caught the relay throw and, grinning like a Cheshire cat, waited for his victims. Gehrig tried to score standing up and smashed into Sewell, but the catcher held on to the ball and tagged him out. Then Sewell dived at Walker and tagged him as well for a shameful double play that wasn't repeated for more than half a century.

THE ONES WHO GOT AWAY

Teams That Foolishly Failed to Hold On to Future Superstars

Baseball owners aren't like fishermen. They don't like to talk about the big ones that got away. More than a few future sluggers and pitching stars have been hooked and then tossed back or allowed to wriggle free. It usually happens because some bait-brain in the front office wouldn't know a prize catch if it jumped up and bit him. For "Teams That Foolishly Failed to Hold On to Future Superstars," The Baseball Hall of SHAME inducts the following:

PIRATES' LOSS OF WALTER JOHNSON
1907

All that stood in the way of putting a Pirates' uniform on Walter Johnson was some cheapskate in the front office. Johnson was getting a lot of attention around the ballparks of the Pacific Northwest with his blazing fastball.

Stunned by the kid's speed and control, a friend of Pittsburgh manager Fred Clarke urged the skipper to bring the pitching sensation east for a tryout. All Johnson needed was a nine-dollar advance for his train fare. Nope, said the front office. No advance for some unknown.

So Walter Johnson missed that train ride. But he did take another trip, to Washington, D.C., where he stayed for 21 years. During that time he pitched an incredible 416 career victories in the American League, the second most in major-league history.

RED SOX' LOSS OF JACKIE ROBINSON
1944

The Boston Red Sox blew a once-in-a-lifetime chance to make history—and, in a way, to make the team stronger. They had first crack at signing Jackie Robinson, but blind with prejudice, they turned him down flat.

To please local civil rights leaders, the Red Sox gave a short tryout to three Negro League stars. One of them was Robinson, a gifted athlete from the Kansas City Monarchs. Boston manager Joe Cronin was impressed by Robinson's awesome fielding and hitting. But management told Jackie that it was against team policy to sign players after so short a tryout. They gave him the old don't-call-us-we'll-call-you routine.

The truth was that the Red Sox didn't want blacks on its team. In fact, they were the last team to integrate and did not do so until 1959, when they signed Pumpsie Green.

Instead of making history with Boston, Robinson broke the color barrier in 1947 with the Brooklyn Dodgers. In his freshman year Robinson led the Dodgers to the pennant and earned baseball's first Rookie of the Year award.

More important, Jackie Robinson opened the door for other blacks to play in the bigs.

REDS' LOSS OF BABE RUTH
1914

If scout Harry Stevens had known anything about baseball, Babe Ruth would have started his major league career with the Cincinnati Reds.

In 1914 Ruth was playing for the Baltimore Orioles of the International League. The team had agreed to allow the Reds to buy any two players from the Orioles' roster. The task of signing them was handed to Stevens—a flunky with no baseball sense. He only had the job because he was a close friend of the Fleischmann family, who owned the Reds.

Stevens watched a few games in Baltimore and made his choice—a really bad one. He failed to see the great potential of Ruth and rejected the power-hitting pitcher. Instead, Stevens signed Claude Derrick and George Twombly. Derrick lasted two games with the Reds, and Twombly batted a lousy .221 over the next three years.

Meanwhile, Ruth went on to become the greatest player the game has ever seen—but not as a member of the Cincinnati Reds.

It's not clear whether Stevens remained a friend of the Fleischmann family.

METS' LOSS OF REGGIE JACKSON
1966

It's no secret that the amateur free-agent draft is like a game of chance, but it can also be an untapped gold mine.

In 1966 the Mets had the first pick in the draft of high school and college players. They took some kid named Steve Chilcott. They passed over a college star named Reggie Jackson, who had been marked for superstardom by almost every major league scout.

Unable to believe their good fortune, the Kansas City A's grabbed the young slugger. Jackson became one of the game's great personalities—an All-Star, the 1973 American League MVP, and a three-time home run champ.

Steve Chilcott never made it to the bigs.

CUBS' LOSS OF JOE DiMAGGIO
1935

During the winter of 1935 Chicago Cubs owner William Wrigley was offered a can't-lose deal. Yet, in his own special way, Wrigley managed to lose.

The deal was offered by Charles Graham, owner of the San Francisco Seals of the Pacific Coast League. He tried to sell Wrigley his young center fielder, Joe DiMaggio, for $25,000. But Wrigley was worried about a knee injury that DiMaggio had suffered the year before.

To solve the problem, Graham told Wrigley he could take DiMaggio on a trial basis. If Wrigley wasn't satisfied after looking DiMaggio over, Graham would take him back and return the whole $25,000.

Even with this no-risk, money-back guarantee, Wrigley still shook his head no. The next year Cub fans shook their heads while DiMaggio tore up the American League with his hitting and launched a Hall of Fame career with the Yankees.

BLIND SPOTS

The Most Flagrantly Blown Calls
by Umpires

Umpires are necessary evils, like batting slumps, bad-hop singles, and cold hot dogs. Without them, what would fans have to gripe about? To be fair, fans must admit that umpires are pretty honest fellows. It's just that the men in blue aren't always right. You'd swear that some of them worked with Seeing Eye dogs. For "The Most Flagrantly Blown Calls by Umpires," The Baseball Hall of SHAME inducts the following:

BILL KLEM
Sept. 27, 1928

Bill Klem's shocking failure to rule interference on a play that unfolded right before his eyes robbed the New York Giants of a chance at the 1928 pennant.

In the last week of the season, the Giants were only

a half game out of first place when they faced the Chicago Cubs. Trailing 3–2 with one out in the sixth inning, New York put runners on second and third.

Batter Shanty Hogan smashed a sharp grounder to pitcher Art Nehf, who wheeled and threw to third baseman Clyde Beck. Andy Reese was the Giant runner on third. He charged for the plate while catcher Gabby Hartnett ran up the line to block Reese. The two collided. Then Hartnett threw his arms around Reese and held him in a bear hug. While Reese wrestled to get free, Beck ran down the line and tagged the runner. It seemed incredible, but Klem ignored the obvious interference and called Reese out.

Within seconds Giants manager John McGraw and his players swarmed around Klem. They hollered and screamed. They rightly charged that Hartnett had interfered, and that Reese should have been allowed to score. But the stubborn Klem refused to listen to reason.

The Giants failed to score in the inning and lost the game, which was played under McGraw's protest. The next day, armed with a *New York Daily News* photograph that showed the interference clearly, McGraw took his case to league president John Heydler. In spite of the proof, Heydler upheld Klem. The Giants were crushed—they went on to lose the pennant.

ART PASSARELLA
Oct. 5, 1952

In the 1952 World Series Art Passarella made such an obviously bad call that even the commissioner of baseball refused to back him up.

It happened in the bottom of the tenth inning of the

Umpire Art Passarella blew a World Series call at first base.

(AP/Wide World Photo)

fifth game between the Brooklyn Dodgers and the New York Yankees. With the score tied 5–5, Yankee pitcher Johnny Sain hit a slow roller to second baseman Jackie Robinson, who threw late to first. But Passarella called Sain out—before the throw even arrived. Sain and coach Bill Dickey both argued loudly, but the umpire stuck by his call. Fired up by the gift, the Dodgers pushed across a run in the top of the eleventh inning and won the game 6–5.

Photos proved without question that Passarella was wrong. When reporters showed Commissioner Ford Frick pictures of the disputed call, he chose not to defend the umpire. Instead Frick said, "If I owned a newspaper, I'd blow that picture up to six columns.''

That's exactly what the *New York Times* did. The giant photo showed that Sain's left foot was firmly on the bag while the ball was still several feet away from the outstretched glove of Dodgers first baseman Gil Hodges.

BILL STEWART
Oct. 6, 1948

National League umpire Bill Stewart was caught flat-footed on a key pickoff play—and he cost the Cleveland Indians the opening game of the 1948 World Series.

Before meeting the Boston Braves in the Series opener, Indians player-manager Lou Boudreau warned the umpiring crew to watch out for his team's timed pickoff play. They had made it work eight times during the year. In the umpires' dressing room Stewart shrugged it off, bragging that he had never been caught off guard by a pickoff play.

Cleveland's Bob Feller and Boston's Johnny Sain hurled shutouts until the bottom of the eighth inning. With the score tied 0–0, the Braves suddenly had runners Phil Masi at second and Sibby Sisti on first.

With two out and Tommy Holmes at bat, shortstop Lou Boudreau hung around second to keep Masi close. But Masi, who represented the winning run, edged off the bag anyway. Then Boudreau touched his knee to signal the pickoff play. All the umpires knew what was about to happen. All except Stewart, that is.

On a count set before the game, Feller wheeled and

fired to second. Boudreau timed the play perfectly. He darted over to the bag, speared the ball, and slapped it on Masi, who was diving back to the base. The pickoff had worked. Everyone—players, fans, and photographers—knew that Masi was nailed for the third out of the inning. But Stewart was surprised and blindly called Masi safe.

Boudreau made a strong protest, but it did no good. Moments later Holmes lashed a single, and Masi streaked around third. Thanks to a free pass from Stewart, Masi crossed the plate with the game's only run. A tainted run.

WELCOME TO THE BIGS!

The Most Disappointing
Major-League Debuts

All baseball players dream about how wonderful their first day in the bigs will be. Some see themselves hammering the winning homer with two out in the bottom of the ninth. Others imagine leaping high against the fence to make a game-saving catch. That's the fantasy. What happens in real life is different. They often stumble over their feet, fall flat on their faces, or embarrass themselves so badly in some other way that it marks them for their whole careers—which can be a lot shorter than they'd planned. For ''The Most Disappointing Major League Debuts,'' The Baseball Hall of SHAME inducts the following:

JOE NUXHALL
Pitcher • Cincinnati, N.L. • June 10, 1944

Joe Nuxhall was so rattled when told to warm up for his first major league game that he tripped over the dugout steps and fell flat on his kisser. It was a sign of things to come—a warning sign.

During the wartime year of 1944 some teams ran short of manpower and had to look under rocks for playing talent. Among them were the Cincinnati Reds, who signed Nuxhall, a 15-year-old ninth grader. Since he was still in school, Nuxhall joined the team on weekends and for a few night games during the week.

On a Saturday afternoon in Crosley Field, the St. Louis Cardinals were creaming the Reds 13–0. Nuxhall was sitting on the bench, watching in starry-eyed wonder, because he had seen so few big-league games. Suddenly he was snapped out of his trance by manager Bill McKechnie, who said, "Go to the bull pen, Joe, and warm up."

The shock of an assignment so soon after signing a contract froze Nuxhall's nerves. He had had no idea he'd get to pitch. He tripped and landed on his face as he headed for the bull pen. The shaken teenager fired several wild balls during his warm-up. But ready or not, the boy wonder took the mound to start the ninth inning, becoming the youngest player ever to appear in the majors.

Nuxhall had walked two and recorded two outs when he came face to face with Stan Musial, the batting champion the year before. Musial ripped a run-scoring single. For a boy who had been pitching against junior high school kids just a few weeks earlier, the pressure was too much. Nuxhall fell apart. He gave up five runs, five walks, two wild pitches, and two hits in two thirds of an inning before McKechnie took mercy on him and took him out of the game.

Two days later Nuxhall was on a train for Birmingham, Alabama, the home of Cincy's farm team in the lowly Sally League.

It was eight years before Nuxhall returned to the majors and recorded his third big-league out.

DOE BOYLAND
First Baseman • Pittsburgh, N.L.
Sept. 4, 1978

In his first major-league at-bat, Pirates rookie Doe Boyland struck out—while sitting on the bench.

In the seventh inning of a home game against the Mets, Pittsburgh manager Chuck Tanner sent Boyland in to pinch-hit for pitcher Ed Wilson. The count was one ball and two strikes when Mets right-handed pitcher Skip Lockwood hurt his arm and had to leave the game.

The Mets switched to southpaw Kevin Kobel. Going by the book, Tanner lifted the left-handed-swinging Boyland and sent right-handed hitter Rennie Stennett in to pinch-hit for the pinch hitter.

Boyland watched sadly from the bench as Stennett struck out on Kobel's first pitch. Under the scoring rules, the strikeout was charged to Boyland.

FRANK VERDI
Shortstop • New York, A.L. • May 10, 1953

Frank Verdi said his first at-bat in the major leagues was "like your first date—it's something you can never forget." But in his case it was like getting stood up.

After spending seven long years in the Yankees' farm system, Verdi finally made the big club. He sat on the bench until that fateful Sunday in Boston's Fenway Park. That was the day he filled in at shortstop for Phil Rizzuto, who had been taken out in the sixth inning for a pinch hitter.

In the top of the seventh Verdi was all set to make his long-awaited first date with the plate. The Yankees had rallied to take a two-run lead and had the bases loaded with two out. What a great moment for Verdi! All the years of suffering in the minors—the sweaty bus rides, the two-bit towns, the fleabag hotels—were about to pay off. Here was his golden opportunity to knock in some important runs in his first big-league at-bat.

Verdi stepped into the batter's box, eager to hit. Then he heard Red Sox coach Bill McKechnie shout, "Time out!" McKechnie sent pitcher Ellis Kinder to the showers and brought in reliever Ken Holcombe. After the new pitcher completed his warm-up tosses, Verdi stepped back into the batter's box.

Once again he heard, "Time out!" This time it was Yankee manager Casey Stengel. Verdi turned around and saw teammate Bill Renna swinging three bats. Stengel was sending him up to pinch-hit for Verdi. That was it for Verdi's debut in the bigs. It was also his final appearance. He was sent back to the minors, never to return.

"At least," he said, "I got into the batter's box twice. A lot of guys only get in once."

LOU STRINGER
Shortstop • Chicago, N.L. • April 14, 1941

Chicago Cubs rookie Lou Stringer grabbed all the headlines in his major-league debut. He even put himself in the record book by committing the most errors— four—of any shortstop on Opening Day.

There was no doubt Stringer was nervous. When the Cubs streaked out of their Wrigley Field dugout for the first inning of the year, he forgot to bring his glove! The embarrassed shortstop ran back to get it.

The glove didn't do him much good. In the first inning Stringer bobbled Pirate Arky Vaughan's grounder and threw wildly to first for an error. In the second inning he let Al Lopez's grounder skip between his legs.

Stringer didn't do any more fielding damage until the ninth inning, when he must have decided the game needed some excitement. The Cubs entered the inning with a 7–2 lead. Then the shaky shortstop made a wild throw and booted what should have been a game-ending double-play ball. With only one out and two runs in, Pittsburgh had the bases loaded and the potential winning run at the plate. But the Cubs survived, 7–4, no thanks to Stringer's disappointing debut.

CAL BROWNING
Pitcher • St. Louis, N.L. • June 12, 1960

Cal Browning's heart was thumping. Just days earlier he had been in the minors, pitching for Rochester. Now, wearing a St. Louis Cardinals uniform, he was about to play in his very first major-league game.

Browning had gone to the mound in relief of veteran Ron Kline. The 22-year-old rookie was already sweating, but it wasn't because of the humid St. Louis heat. It was because he was a nervous wreck.

Into the batter's box stepped crafty hitter Don Hoak, third baseman for the Pittsburgh Pirates. As he finished his warm-up tosses, Browning remembered the book on Hoak—pitch him high inside fastballs.

Browning checked the two runners on base. Then he went into his stretch and let fly his very first major-league pitch. Whack! Hoak's bat caught every bit of the high inside fastball and sent it rocketing over the wall at Busch Stadium for a home run.

It wasn't just a normal four-bagger either. Browning's first pitch turned into a gopher ball that was hit so hard it busted the red neon eagle in the Budweiser sign on the left-field scoreboard.

Browning never recovered from the shock. He walked the next batter and gave up four more hits and two more runs in two thirds of an inning before he was yanked.

Cardinals manager Solly Hemus had seen enough. He shipped Browning back to Rochester, and the dazed left-hander never pitched in the majors again.

The Most Pitiful
Pitching Performances

You can always spot the lousy pitchers. Their curves hang longer than punts, while their fastballs move slower than balloons on a still day. Even so, they play an important role in baseball—they fatten batting averages. For "The Most Pitiful Pitching Performances," The Baseball Hall of SHAME inducts the following:

HARLEY "DOC" PARKER
Cincinnati, N.L. • June 21, 1901

Doc Parker asked for a second chance as a pitcher so he could leave his mark on baseball. He got his chance. And he left his mark—a bad one.

Parker hurled the worst-pitched ballgame in major-league history.

After three years as a pitcher for the Chicago Cubs,

he had a so-so won-loss record. Dropped from the roster after the 1896 season, Parker left the major-league scene for five long years. Then, suddenly, he showed up at the doorstep of the seventh-place Cincinnati Reds.

Parker wanted to pitch again, and they needed help. As it turned out, Parker didn't solve their pitching problems. He made them worse.

In his new Cincinnati uniform Parker went to the mound and threw batting practice. Only this time it wasn't practice. It was a major-league game against the Brooklyn Dodgers, the previous year's champions. Actually, it didn't matter who faced him. Anybody with a bat could have hit Parker's pitches.

Parker gave up a homer, five doubles, and 20 singles. Every player who stepped up to the plate smacked a hit. In fact, the Dodgers were so eager to fatten their batting averages that they ran to the plate. But Reds manager John McPhee showed no mercy and left Parker in the game for a whipping.

Brooklyn scored at will in every inning, ripping 26 hits and tallying 21 runs. By the eighth inning they grew tired of running the bases, so they just tapped at the ball halfheartedly. In its story on the game the *Brooklyn Daily Eagle* said that the Dodgers "allowed themselves to be retired without attempting to run out the hits, which were fielded slowly and painfully by the tired and weary Cincinnatis."

When he staggered off the mound at game's end, Parker had set two pitching records that still stand—a National League mark for most runs given up and a major-league record for most hits allowed.

The next day there was a short notice at the bottom

of the *Daily Eagle* sports page: "The Cincinnati Reds announced they released Harley 'Doc' Parker today."

CHUCK STOBBS
Washington, A.L. • May 20, 1956

Chuck Stobbs uncorked one of the wildest pitches in major-league history. It was a "tape measure" throw that sailed 30 feet toward the first-base side of home plate—and landed 17 rows up in the stands.

The Washington Senators left-hander was pitching a shutout in the bottom of the fourth inning against the Detroit Tigers. But with one out he gave up two hits and a walk to load the bases.

Stobbs didn't want to give batter Bob Kennedy anything good to hit. The hurler had no reason to worry. He wound up and unleashed a pitch that was so wild it crossed two time zones and was tracked by radar. It cost him a run as each of the runners happily moved up 90 feet.

"I was so surprised," recalled Stobbs, who lost the game 4–2. "I didn't know if I should dig a hole and try to hide under the mound or what to do. All I could do was stand there and wait for the umpire to throw me a new ball."

How did it happen?

"As I was winding up, I hit myself on the side of the leg so the ball was right on my fingertips. There was nothing else I could do except go ahead and throw the ball, and that's where it ended up.

"Nobody said much to me when I came off the mound. They knew better."

HUGH "LOSING PITCHER" MULCAHY
Philadelphia–Pittsburgh, N.L. • 1935–40, 1945–47

There wasn't any one thing about Hugh Mulcahy's pitching that was really bad—other than his won-loss record. How else could a guy earn the nickname "Losing Pitcher"?

The Philadelphia sportswriters were never known for being kind to the Phillies. But they stuck Mulcahy with a label that he never lived down. In those days newspapers received out-of-town game scores on a Western Union ticker line. Because Mulcahy lost two out of every three games (45–89), the ticker line score of his games most often ended with "Losing pitcher—Mulcahy." After a while whenever he appeared on the mound a chant went up in the press box: "Now pitching for Philadelphia, Losing Pitcher Mulcahy."

Part of his trouble was that he pitched for a terrible team. During his years with the Phillies they needed to climb a ladder to see the bottom of the league.

Mulcahy had another problem, though. He didn't start out as a pitcher. He was really a shortstop. But his long legs got mixed up with ground balls, and his hits were as common as Philadelphia's pennant-winning years. On the other hand, he was big, and he had a strong arm.

Mulcahy was given a tryout as a pitcher in front of Phillies manager Jimmy Wilson. After watching Mulcahy throw, Wilson shook his head, turned to his assistant, and said, "Doesn't know how to stand on the rubber, doesn't know how to throw his fastball, and has no idea of control."

Before joining the army, Hugh Mulcahy earned a new nickname that stuck forever—Losing Pitcher.

(AP/Wide World Photo)

In a move that helps explain the Phillies' record back then, Wilson signed Mulcahy up as a pitcher. Tossing him into game after game, Wilson told Mulcahy, "You'll have to learn your lessons losing."

Mulcahy tried to do what he was told—learn by losing. He never did enjoy a winning season. During an awful stretch from 1937 to 1940 Mulcahy suffered four losing seasons in a row: 8–18, 10–20, 9–16, and 13–22. The 1940 season was a real heartbreaker. On July 31 he owned a 12–10 record and was sure he would finally shed his embarrassing nickname. In fact, he set his sights on winning 20 games. He pitched with all his heart—and lost 12 straight games. In his last start of the year he finally broke the streak. He ended that season with the most defeats of any pitcher—22.

To make matters worse, he got drafted. He could have delayed going, but he didn't. He figured he'd take a year off from baseball and come back with new energy to improve his record. So he joined the army on March 8, 1941.

But "Losing Pitcher" was true to his name. Three months before he was due to come home, the United States declared war on Japan. Without meaning to, Mulcahy became the first big leaguer to enter World War II—and one of the last to get out.

TOM GORMAN   MARK FREEMAN
GEORGE BRUNET
Kansas City, A.L. • April 22, 1959

It was the sorriest show of pitching control ever seen in one inning.

Kansas City A's hurlers Tom Gorman, Mark Freeman, and George Brunet were so wild they couldn't find home plate with a road map.

In one terrible inning the struggling pitchers walked 10 batters and hit another. They allowed the visiting Chicago White Sox to score 11 runs *on only one single*. What's worse, eight of those runs were forced in by bases-loaded walks. For this reason, the A's performance is even more shameful than that of the Washington Senators' record-setting 11 free passes in one inning on September 11, 1949.

The White Sox were winning 8–6 in the seventh inning when a hit and three errors brought in two runs and put a runner on third base. Gorman could have suffered less harm if the strike zone had been high and outside. But it wasn't, and he started the pitiful base-on-balls procession.

Gorman walked two batters in a row to load the bases and then threw two straight balls to the next hitter.

Manager Harry Craft yanked Gorman and brought in Freeman. Whatever pitching disease Gorman had was caught by Freeman. Surrounded by White Sox, Freeman tossed two more balls, which finished the walk and forced in the third run. Then he gave away two free passes—with a force-out at home in between— for another two tallies.

Brunet came in to relieve. Keeping up the pace set by his teammates, Brunet forced in the final six runs with a walk, walk, hit batsman (to break up the boredom), walk, strikeout (no big deal, it was the opposing pitcher), walk, walk, and an inning-ending groundout.

Seventeen White Sox came to the plate in the half-inning walkathon that lasted 45 minutes. The A's

were out in the field so long they could have planted
and grown corn.

The final score: White Sox 20, A's 6.

PAUL LaPALME
Chicago, A.L. • May 18, 1957

Paul LaPalme had the easiest pitching job ever given
to a hurler. Just hold the ball. That's all, just hold the
ball.

It's incredible, but he didn't. And he blew the game.

The Chicago White Sox were winning 4–3 over the
Baltimore Orioles when LaPalme went out to the
mound in the bottom of the ninth inning. His manager, Al Lopez, gave him a strict and simple instruction
—stall.

Under an agreement made before the game, the
umpires were to halt play at exactly 10:20 P.M. so the
Sox could catch a train for Boston. It was 10:18 P.M.
when Oriole Dick Williams led off the ninth inning.
Unable to think of any smart way to stall, LaPalme
threw a strike and a ball.

By now time was almost up. In just a few seconds
the White Sox could leave town as winners. All
LaPalme had to do was stand there. Or tie his shoe-
laces. Or scratch his head. Or pick his nose. He could
do anything but throw the ball.

LaPalme threw the ball anyway—and not way outside, or into the ground or any other spot that would
have made a hit impossible. No, Paul LaPalme threw
the ball right down the pipe, and Dick Williams
whacked it with all his might. As the minute hand
stroked exactly 10:20 P.M., the ball landed high in the

left-field bleachers for a dramatic game-tying homer. The umps then called the game with the score knotted at 4–4.

Lopez blew his top like a volcano. He ranted and raved and stormed into the clubhouse as the White Sox scattered. They had never seen their leader so angry.

Under American League rules, the tie meant the whole game had to be replayed at a later date. When it was, the Orioles won the rematch.

As for LaPalme, his time ran out. After that year he never played in the majors again.

THE FALL FOLLIES

The Worst World Series Performances

The World Series isn't always all that it's cracked up to be. Of course, the lords of baseball want everybody to believe that the October super-event shows off the two best teams in the game, with fantastic fielding, thrilling baserunning, dynamite hitting, and awesome pitching. In truth, the Fall Classic is often the Classic Fall—from grace to disgrace for so-called champions. For "The Worst World Series Performances," The Baseball Hall of SHAME inducts the following:

ROGER PECKINPAUGH
Shortstop • Washington, A.L. • 1925

On the night before the 1925 World Series Roger Peckinpaugh was named the American League's Most Valuable Player. It was a real feather in his cap. But he couldn't wear the cap for long. The goat horns he sprouted in the Series grew much too large.

Roger Peckinpaugh pecked and pawed his way to a record eight errors in one World Series.

(National Baseball Library)

Peckinpaugh set a record that no butterfingered Hall of Shamer has come close to matching. He pecked and pawed his way to eight errors in one World Series.

Playing as if his glove were made of cement, the worst fielder in the history of the Fall Classic fumbled away three games. As a result the Pittsburgh Pirates came from behind to win the world championship right out from under the noses of the stunned Washington Senators.

Peck's Bad Boy ranged to his right, and to his left, and deep in the hole to bungle balls throughout the Series.

He blew the second game in the eighth inning. With the score knotted at 1–1, Peckinpaugh bobbled Eddie Moore's easy grounder. Moments later Kiki Cuyler belted a homer, scoring Moore ahead of him as the Pirates won 3–2.

In the sixth game Peckinpaugh's bungling wiped out a 2–0 Washington lead. After Eddie Moore walked in the third inning Max Carey hit a double-play ball to Peckinpaugh, but he booted it, leaving both runners safe. A sacrifice, an infield out (which would have been the third out of the inning), and a single drove home two unearned runs. The Pirates won 3–2 again— this time to even the Series.

It didn't seem possible that Peckinpaugh could play any worse, but he did. In the deciding game Washington held a 6–4 lead in the seventh inning. Once again Peckinpaugh came down with the dropsies. Moore hit a high pop-up to him, and Peckinpaugh was ready to make a routine catch—routine for most fielders anyway. He muffed it. Pittsburgh followed his error with a double and a triple to tie the score at 6–6.

In the top of the eighth, however, Peckinpaugh smashed a homer to give the Senators a 7–6 lead. Would Peck make up for his monstrous mistakes? Nope.

With two out in the bottom of the eighth Pittsburgh tied the game with back-to-back doubles. Then Moore walked, and Carey rapped an easy grounder to Peckinpaugh. He scooped it up, but as he ran to touch second for the easy force-out on Moore, Peckinpaugh stumbled. He dropped the ball for his eighth error. This one filled the bases. The stage was set for Cuyler, who quickly doubled home the two winning runs. The Pirates won the Series with a 9–7 victory, thanks to Peckinpaugh's four unearned runs.

Needless to say, there was no dinner in Washington in honor of Peckinpaugh's MVP award.

CURT FLOOD
Outfielder • St. Louis, N.L. • Oct. 10, 1968

Curt Flood belongs to the Meat Cutter's Union for the way he butchered the St. Louis Cardinals' bid for the 1968 world championship.

In a scoreless duel in the seventh game against the Detroit Tigers, Flood wrote his name twice in the World Series book of bozos.

The first screw-up came in the sixth inning, after Flood beat out an infield hit. He was on first base with the potential winning run, but he got picked off like a tin can hit by a sharpshooter. He should have been ready for it, because teammate Lou Brock had been picked off earlier in the inning. Flood's lame postgame excuse? "I just didn't think he'd throw over to first."

But the folly for which Flood will long be famous took place in the seventh inning. With the score still tied at 0–0, he misjudged a fly ball to center. Detroit had two on and two out when Jim Northrup hit a line drive that was well within Flood's reach. Flood took three quick steps in, then stepped on the brakes and changed directions. He retreated toward the wall, but it was too late. The ball sailed over his head for a cheap triple, and the two winning runs crossed the plate. Moments later Northrup scored. That's all the Tigers needed. They went on to whip the Cardinals 4–1 for the world championship.

No truer words were spoken when Flood said, "What it all amounts to is I fouled up."

AARON WARD
Second Baseman • New York, A.L. • Oct. 13, 1921

Aaron Ward ran for glory, but he made a wrong turn.

In the bottom of the ninth inning of the final game of the World Series, the New York Giants had a slim 1–0 lead over the Yankees. With one out, Ward walked. Now he represented the tying run for the Yanks. Ward wanted to make something happen. He did. He made something bad happen.

Teammate Frank Baker slashed a hard grounder. Second baseman Johnny Rawlings snared it on his knees and got up in time to nail Baker at first by an eyelash. Meanwhile, Ward roared around second base like a kamikaze pilot and headed for third. Even a rookie knows better than to risk the third out by trying to advance two bases on an infield out. But Ward was no rookie. He was no speed demon either, having stolen only six bases the whole year.

First baseman George Kelly rifled a throw to third

baseman Frankie Frisch, who slapped the easy tag on Ward. Third out. End of game. End of Series. End of a stupid play.

MAX FLACK   PHIL DOUGLAS
Outfielder   Pitcher
Chicago, N.L. • Sept. 9, 1918

Flack & Douglas. It sounds like a wrecking company. It *was* a wrecking company. The two Chicago Cubs crushed their own team's chances of winning the crucial fourth game of the World Series.

Chicago was behind the Boston Red Sox two games to one. A win would even the Series; a loss would put the Cubs in a deep hole. By the time Flack & Douglas were finished, the Cubs were as good as buried.

Flack started the demolition derby in the first inning. He singled but was picked off when catcher Sam Agnew caught him napping. In the third inning Flack got picked off again. This time it was at second base, by pitcher Babe Ruth.

Playing right field, Flack led the Cubs to even more ruin in the fourth inning. With two out, Boston put runners on second and third, bringing the ever-dangerous Babe Ruth up to bat. Chicago pitcher George Tyler waved at Flack to move back toward the fence. Flack moved only a few inches. Again, Tyler waved to Flack to play deeper, but the hardheaded outfielder still refused.

Even though Ruth spent part of the year as a starting pitcher, he still led the league in homers. None of that mattered to Flack. It should have mattered. Ruth clobbered Tyler's next pitch, and the ball sailed over

Flack's head. By the time Flack tracked down the ball, Ruth had reached third with a stand-up triple. Even worse, the Red Sox had a 2–0 lead. If Flack had listened to his pitcher and played deep, he could have caught Ruth's drive. It would have been the third out, and Boston wouldn't have scored.

The next time Ruth came to bat, in the seventh inning, Flack did play deep. He played so deep he needed a bleacher ticket. The crowd in Boston got a good laugh at his expense when he had to dash in to catch Ruth's sacrifice fly.

In the eighth inning the Cubs tied the score at 2–2, but with no help from Flack. He grounded out as runners held at second and third.

Relief pitcher Phil Douglas finished what Flack had started doing to his team. Shufflin' Phil came into the tie game in the bottom of the eighth. As soon as he did, he gave up a single to Wally Schang, who then scooted to second on a passed ball.

With the winning run in scoring position, Douglas went to his special pitch—the spitter. He threw it to Harry Hooper, who laid down a nifty bunt. When Douglas fielded the ball it was so wet from his spit that he lost his grip and threw wildly past first base. Schang raced home easily with the winning run.

Wrote the *New York Times,* "The trickery pitching of Douglas had turned on him like a boomerang, and he succumbed to his own faulty artfulness."

And thus the company of Flack & Douglas helped complete the fourth-game demolition of the Chicago Cubs.

BACKSTOP BLOCKHEADS

The Most Bungled Plays by Catchers

The catcher's mask, chest protector, and shin guards are called the "tools of ignorance" for a good reason. Anybody with an ounce of brains knows better than to squat for 2½ hours behind the plate getting whacked by foul tips, trying to stop 100 mph fastballs, and being bowled over by base runners. For "The Most Bungled Plays by Catchers," The Baseball Hall of SHAME inducts the following:

HANK GOWDY
New York, N.L. • Oct. 10, 1924

As graceful as Hank Gowdy was in the seventh and final game of the 1924 Series, the Giants catcher probably would have tripped over his own shadow. His clumsiness cost his team the world championship.

Gowdy was behind the plate in the bottom of the twelfth inning of a 3–3 tie. Up to bat for the Washington Senators stepped weak-hitting Muddy Ruel, who had managed to get only two hits in 21 trips to the plate during the Series.

Muddy lifted a high, lazy foul back of the plate for what looked like an easy out. Like a good catcher, Gowdy threw off his mask and went after the pop-up. But, like a bad catcher, he threw his mask right in his own path.

As he circled under the foul, Gowdy pulled a boner seldom seen in baseball. He stepped on his mask and got his foot stuck. Keeping his eye on the ball, he tried with all his might to shake off the discarded hardware. By now the ball was dropping, and Gowdy was panicking. Looking as if he were doing a poor imitation of Long John Silver, Gowdy hobbled on his mask and stumbled as the ball dropped harmlessly beside him.

Fired up by the second chance at the plate that Gowdy had given him, Ruel rapped a sharp double. Earl McNeely then hit a bad-hop single, and Ruel raced home with the winning run—and the world championship.

BOB TILLMAN
Boston, A.L. • May 12, 1967

Bob Tillman spent hours practicing throws to second base so he could shoot down thieving runners. He didn't mow down all that many base stealers, but he did manage to nail his own pitcher.

Boston Red Sox relief pitcher John Wyatt had come in to pitch in the eighth inning of a tight game against the visiting Detroit Tigers. Fans gave him an ovation because he had yet to be scored on in eight appearances that year.

Wyatt walked Al Kaline, who broke for second base two pitches later. Tillman cut loose with a strong throw as Wyatt ducked and turned toward second to see how good his catcher's marksmanship was. The pitcher learned that it was painfully off target.

The throw struck Wyatt smack in the back of his head! The ball bounced all the way to the on-deck circle on the first-base side of the field. As the amazed fans watched in horror Wyatt staggered around on the mound. By the time Tillman got the ball back, Kaline had reached third base.

Tillman was charged with an error, and Wyatt ended up with a headache. But the plucky pitcher stayed in the game. The next batter, Willie Horton, hit a sacrifice fly for the first run of the year off Wyatt. The run was not only unearned but also crucial: The Red Sox lost 5–4.

Not in recent memory had anyone seen a catcher throw a beanball at a pitcher.

AARON ROBINSON
Detroit, A.L. • Sept. 24, 1950

In the final week of the 1950 season, the Tigers still had a chance to knock the mighty Yankees out of first place. But Detroit's pennant dream was derailed when Aaron Robinson fell asleep at the switch.

The Tigers were only two games behind New York when they came into Cleveland's Municipal Stadium to play the Indians. The game turned into a classic pitchers' duel and went into the bottom of the tenth inning tied 1–1.

Aaron Robinson's mental blunder helped eliminate his team from the pennant race.

(George Brace Photo)

Indians pitcher Bob Lemon led off the inning with a booming triple. Tigers manager Red Rolfe had no choice but to order pitcher Ted Gray to walk the next two batters intentionally and load the bases for a possible force-out at home.

Cleveland's Larry Doby then hit a pop-up for the first out. The next batter, Luke Easter, hit a grounder to first baseman Don Kolloway. He fielded the ball, stepped on the bag for the second out, and then threw home, hoping to complete a game-saving double play.

Lemon, coming from third, was a good five feet from home when Robinson took the throw and stepped on the plate. It was incredible, but Robinson made no attempt to tag the runner as he should have because Kolloway, by stepping on first base before throwing home, had taken off the force.

Robinson just stood there like a rock as Lemon slid across the plate at the catcher's feet for the winning run.

The shocking loss helped eliminate the Tigers from the pennant race. But it came as no surprise when Robinson was traded the following year.

PAUL RATLIFF
Minnesota, A.L. • April 25, 1970

The very first rule a catcher learns is that on a dropped third strike he must tag the batter or throw to first. Twins catcher Paul Ratliff must have played hooky when that lesson was taught. His blunder allowed a Detroit batter to reach third on a strikeout.

It happened in a game against the Tigers during Ratliff's rookie season. He trapped the ball in the dirt after Detroit's Earl Wilson swung and missed for a third strike. But Ratliff did not tag Wilson. Thinking it was the third out, Ratliff rolled the ball back toward the mound and ran into the dugout while the rest of his team started running off the field.

George Resinger, who was coaching at third for the Tigers, spotted the boo-boo. He waited until most of the Twins were in the dugout and then yelled at Wilson to run. Hardly the fastest human afoot, Wilson made it to first easily. Since the Twins weren't watching, he lumbered to second and then headed for third. Twins left fielder Brant Alyea, who was slowly trotting in, suddenly realized that Wilson was trying to score. Alyea ran to the mound, picked up the ball, and shouted for help. Wilson was around third when Alyea threw to shortstop Leo Cardenas, who had raced out of the dugout to cover home. Then Alyea ran to cover third.

Unfortunately for Detroit, Wilson suddenly pulled a hamstring muscle and was tagged out by Alyea on Cardenas's return throw.

On his way back to catcher's school, Ratliff said, "I didn't know you had to tag the runner in that case."

JOHNNY PEACOCK
Boston, A.L. • Sept. 12, 1942

Johnny Peacock was conked on the head because he didn't use his brain.

The embarrassing—and painful—moment occurred in the bottom of the eighth inning as his Boston Red Sox held a slim 4–3 lead over the Cleveland Indians. When the Tribe put runners on first and second, Peacock decided to switch signals with his pitcher Joe Dobson so the runner on second would have trouble stealing the signs.

But Peacock forgot one important thing. He failed to tell Dobson he had switched the signals.

Behind the plate Peacock flashed one finger, which to him now meant curveball. But to Dobson it was still the same fastball signal they had been using the whole game.

While Peacock moved his glove low in expectation of a curveball, Dobson fired a blazing fastball right in the strike zone. Unable to get his mitt up in time, Peacock was nailed smack in the head. The ball bounced off his forehead and bounded to the screen behind home plate. Peacock staggered after the ball while players in both dugouts reeled with laughter.

It wasn't funny to Peacock. He suffered a throbbing headache. That was quite understandable, in view of Dobson's remark to reporters after the game: "That pitch was my very best fast one."

DAVE ENGLE
Minnesota, A.L. • May 15, 1984

Minnesota Twins catcher Dave Engle caught what he thought was a nifty shutout. But he left his position a wee bit too soon.

With one out in the top of the ninth inning and the Twins ahead 1–0, the Toronto Blue Jays had runners on first and second. Then pinch hitter Rick Leach hit what seemed to be a game-ending double-play grounder. But first baseman Kent Hrbek dropped the relay throw. Meanwhile, Blue Jay runner Mitch Webster steamed from second base around third and headed for home. Hrbek then threw to the plate, but no one was there.

Where was Engle? He was out on the mound congratulating relief pitcher Ron Davis! A little too soon.

Because the catcher had deserted his post, Hrbek's throw sailed to the backstop, and the tying run scored. Toronto went on to win 5–2 in ten innings.

A rather ashamed Engle said after the game, "I went out to congratulate Ron Davis. I took my eye off the umpire. Then I heard everybody screaming, and I couldn't figure out what it was all about. I turned around and saw the ball was going back to home plate."

Engle was in no mood to hear what Toronto catcher Buck Martinez had to say about the chuckleheaded play: "You just can't take anything for granted in this game. Sooner or later it will catch up with you, and you'll get embarrassed."

HEAVE HO-HO'S

The Most Embarrassing Ejections
from a Game

Although umpires don't see all the things they should, they usually manage to hear all the things they shouldn't. What comes next are heated arguments that end when umps thumb their attackers out of the game. However, this routine sometimes takes a weird turn and ends up looking like a circus sideshow. For "The Most Embarrassing Ejections from a Game," The Baseball Hall of SHAME inducts the following:

THE VOICE
July 19, 1946

A ventriloquist in the stands who made his heckling sound as if it was coming from the dugout caused 14 innocent Chicago White Sox players to be thrown out of a game.

Umpire Red Jones ejected every player and coach in the White Sox dugout.

(AP/Wide World Photo)

The Voice baffled umpire Red Jones and started one of the biggest group evictions in baseball history.

Jones was behind the plate in Boston when he accused Chicago pitcher Joe Haynes of throwing a beanball at Ted Williams. Then the ventriloquist went into action.

Jones heard one too many zingers come from what he thought was the dugout. So he threw out Ralph Hodgin, one of the team's quietest players. But The Voice would not be silenced, and players joined in the heckling. Three more White Sox were tossed out, but The Voice kept hollering insults from the shadows of the dugout. Even after the abused Jones ejected his fifth player of the day, there was no relief for him.

The bench jockeying, led by The Voice, had driven the umpire over the edge. In a panic Jones ordered the entire bench cleared of the nine players and coaches who were left. As they paraded from their dugout to the clubhouse runway on the first-base side, each of them had some choice words for the poor umpire.

"Take these," said coach Bing Miller, offering his glasses to Jones. "You need 'em more than I do."

With an empty Chicago dugout, Jones was free of harassment. Or so he thought. Suddenly, Jones heard, "Hey, meathead, let's see some hustle before the home folks!" It was The Voice.

TOM GORMAN
Umpire • July 1, 1963

National League umpire Tom Gorman deserved the thumb—for throwing out the wrong player on purpose.

Gorman was calling balls and strikes in a game in Philadelphia when one of the Phillies started blasting him from the dugout. Gorman was pelted with remarks such as "Where's your Seeing Eye dog?" and "Why don't you punch a hole in your mask?" The heckler wouldn't let up, and by the seventh inning Gorman had taken enough guff.

Not knowing who the heckler was, the ump decided to take a shot at somebody. He chose third baseman Don Hoak, who had had a run-in with him the previous week. Besides, Gorman figured, it wouldn't hurt the team much because Hoak had a leg injury and wasn't even playing.

Pointing toward the corner of the dugout where he thought he had spotted Hoak, Gorman shouted, "Okay, Hoak, you're out of there!"

Phillies manager Gene Mauch rushed to the plate in protest. "Why are you picking on my players? So far you've been working a pretty good game, not bad for you. You've only missed six or seven pitches so far."

"Don't play around with me," said Gorman. "Get that donkey Hoak out of the dugout."

Mauch put his hands on his hips and pushed his face to within inches of the umpire's. "Let me tell you something," snapped Mauch. "Hoak isn't in the dugout. He's in the bull pen." The bull pen was 380 feet away. "What are you going to do now?"

Trying hard not to turn red from embarrassment, Gorman replied, "Get him over here."

Mauch waved to the bull pen, and Hoak jogged in, thinking he was going to pinch-hit. When Mauch told him, "Gorman just put you out," Hoak started ranting and raving and jumping up and down. But Gorman would not be swayed. He tossed Hoak out.

The next day Hoak bumped into Gorman in the clubhouse runway leading to the field. "Answer me one thing, Tom," said Hoak. "How did you know I was hollering down in the bull pen?"

DOUG ZIMMER   AL FRIEDMAN
Cameramen • Sports Channel • May 9, 1984

Cable TV cameramen Doug Zimmer and Al Friedman proved that television has no place in the dugout.

They were booted out of a game by umpire Joe West for breaking a golden rule of broadcasting. They showed a controversial replay to several players during a game.

Zimmer and Friedman were covering the Mets-Braves game at Shea Stadium for the Sports Channel. They slipped down to the corner of the New York dugout to get better shots for the viewers. From that angle the cameramen followed Mets baserunner Hubie Brooks as he tried to score from second base on a single in the fourth inning. West called Brooks out at the plate.

Manager Davey Johnson was furious at the call and argued loudly with West, but it didn't help. Meanwhile, back in the dugout, coach Bobby Valentine and pitcher Mike Torrez huddled in front of the Sports Channel camera monitor. Zimmer and Friedman showed an instant replay of the action.

What the Mets saw on TV made them even angrier. They let West know that he'd blown the play. In return, West let the two TV cameramen know they had blown their welcome. In a move that made sure he wouldn't win any Emmys, West threw Zimmer and Friedman out of the game.

The next day the Mets management called National League president Chub Feeney to complain about West's thumb. Feeney explained that while it had never happened before, it's against the rules to show replays to players on the bench. So West was right to pull the plug on the TV boys.

EARL WEAVER
Manager • Baltimore, A.L. • Sept. 29, 1985

Managers Mel Ott, Billy Martin, and Earl Weaver were all given the old heave-ho twice in a doubleheader. But only Weaver got his second thumb of the day *before* the start of the nightcap.

The ejections were the 92nd and 93rd in the career of the hotheaded Baltimore Orioles skipper.

Weaver went on the warpath in the first inning of the first game of a doubleheader at Yankee Stadium. For ten minutes he argued with plate umpire Nick Bremigan over a foul ball. In the second inning Weaver went into a seven-minute tantrum over a dropped third strike.

In the third inning the quick-tempered manager charged out of the dugout again to question a call. Bremigan had seen more than enough of Weaver. "You're gone!" the ump shouted. "You've been out here too much today."

But Weaver refused to leave the field. Umpiring crew chief Jim Evans pulled out a stopwatch and told Weaver, "You're wasting time." The fuming manager grabbed the watch and hurled it into the Oriole dugout. "I would have thrown the watch into the stands if I had a better arm," said Weaver. "But my arm isn't what it used to be."

As Weaver stormed off the field, one of the umpires yelled at him, "Go back home and play golf, Earl. The game has passed you by."

Spending the rest of the game in the clubhouse did not improve Weaver's mood. The "Earl of Balti-

Earl Weaver blew up in another argument with an umpire before getting thumbed out of the game.

(New York Daily News Photo)

more" was still spitting fire when he handed in the lineup card before the start of the second game. At home plate he told Evans that after the first-game ejection, Orioles second baseman Rich Dauer had heard the ump say, "I want to meet Weaver in the parking lot after the game." (Most likely it was to discuss baseball—with his fists.)

Evans denied he had ever made such a threat. Then, in a voice that grew more angry with every word, Evans snarled at Weaver, "You're free to go to the parking lot right now, 'cause you're outta here!" For the second time that day Weaver got the boot.

To cap off this sorry moment in history, Weaver kicked dirt on Evans. Then he scooped up a big handful of dirt and threw it at the ump. Because of his behavior Weaver was suspended for three days—the sixth suspension of his career.

That wasn't the first time that Weaver was ejected twice in one game. In a doubleheader on August 15, 1975, the bickering manager was thumbed out by umpire Ron Luciano during the first game and then again before the start of the nightcap.

"Weaver is like a nightmare that keeps coming back," declared Nick Bremigan.

Razing the Roof

The Worst Ballparks
for Watching and Playing Games

The boring, round, all-purpose stadiums where most teams play today are totally drab and dull. They're nothing like the ballparks built before domes, artificial turf, and theater seats. The old ballparks had style, color, and charm. Oh, yeah? Many were or are just as bad as the new ones. Some must have been built by people who hated baseball, because inside these torture chambers fans and players alike have frozen, fried, and risked life and limb. For "The Worst Ballparks for Watching and Playing Games," The Baseball Hall of SHAME inducts the following:

FENWAY PARK
Boston • 1912–Present

Fenway is a nice place to visit, but you wouldn't want to play there. Teams don't just battle each other—they also fight the sun, the wind, the fog, the pigeons, and the terrible Green Monster.

This stadium looks innocent, but it boasts one of the most brutal sun fields in baseball. In Boston it's said that the sun rises in the east and sets in the eyes of the right fielder.

Actually the sun blinds everybody. In late September 1972 the Red Sox started an important game against Detroit by losing the first two fly balls the Tigers hit in the sun. That same year a high hopper hit Chicago White Sox pitcher Wilbur Wood in the knee because he was blinded by the sun.

The weather at Fenway is often terrible. New England gale winds have blown pop flies into homers, torn the big hand off the old center-field clock, and bent the left-field foul pole. On April 25, 1962, the gusty east wind dropped the temperature at Fenway from 78 degrees to 58 degrees in ten minutes.

When the winds die down the fog often rolls in as thick as clam chowder. On August 8, 1966, the game had to be stopped four times because of poor visibility.

Mother Nature abuses players in other ways, too. She gives pigeons and sea gulls one-way tickets to Fenway. On May 17, 1947, St. Louis Browns hurler Ellis Kinder was bombed when a sea gull dropped a three-ounce fish on the mound.

But pigeons are Fenway's national bird. In 1974 Detroit slugger Willie Horton mortally wounded a pigeon with a foul fly near home plate. In 1945 a Fenway pigeon got in the way of a throw from Athletics outfielder Hal Peck on a double by Boston's Skeeter Newsome. The pigeon lost some feathers. The A's lost the game.

That same season Boston outfielder Tom McBride took a bead on what he felt sure was a long fly off the bat of Philadelphia's Sam Chapman. Too late, McBride realized he'd been chasing a pigeon.

If Ted Williams had had his way, there would have been very few pigeons to squawk about. After a game in 1940 he grabbed a shotgun and blasted about 40 of the dirty birds out of the sky. But the Humane Society swooped down on him with a severe reprimand.

The weather and the birds haven't affected the way baseball is played at Fenway as much as the Green Monster has. This 37-foot-high wall, topped by a 23-foot screen, looms just 315 feet from the plate to the left-field foul pole.

What would be a routine fly in most parks can turn into a home run over the Fenway screen. But rising line drives that would soar out of other parks just dent the Green Monster, going for doubles, and sometimes only singles.

HUBERT H. HUMPHREY METRODOME
Minneapolis • 1982–Present

"It's a travesty," said Toronto manager Bobby Cox. "Hit the ball on the ground and it bounces over your head. Hit it in the air and you can't see it."

"It's the worst place ever," swore Baltimore outfielder Fred Lynn.

"This place stinks," complained Yankees manager Billy Martin. "It's a shame it was named after a great guy like Humphrey."

Those are some of the nicer things said about the Metrodome, the indoor playground of the Minnesota Twins.

Whoever designed the Dome had a weird sense of humor. Baseballs bounce like tennis balls on the SuperTurf. High pop-ups get trapped in the low ceiling. Players lose sight of balls against the gray-white background. Fans in the upper deck in left field get their fannies fried by the heat from the scoreboard.

It's the only stadium that ever drew an official protest. After letting two easy pop-ups drop because they couldn't see them, the Yankees played the next game at the Metrodome under protest. On May 8, 1985, manager Billy Martin charged that the Dome wasn't up to major-league standards and should be banned from baseball. The protest was denied.

In a June 1985 game Twins second baseman Tim Teufel hit a simple 150-foot fly that turned into a cheap inside-the-park homer. When it fell on the SuperTurf, it bounced over the head of Chicago White Sox right fielder Harold Baines.

To be fair, some changes were made before the 1985 All-Star Game. But until then the lights were too bright on the right side and too dim on the left side. Grumbling about the glare, Twins right fielder Tom Brunansky wore sunglasses in the outfield. It was strange to see in an indoor stadium.

Blue Jays shortstop Alfredo Griffin lost a hopper over the mound in the lights, which prompted his coach Bob Didier to say, "Only in Minnesota could someone lose a ground ball in the lights during the day."

Still, the Metrodome's low ceiling has led to some high drama. In a game against Oakland on May 4, 1984, A's slugger Dave Kingman hit a sky-high pop-up over the pitcher's mound. The ball never came down. It went through an eight-inch hole in the fabric roof about 180 feet above home plate. Kingman collected a ground-rule double.

From the fans' point of view, the Dome is boring and built to stay that way. Even National Guard armories have more appeal than the Dome.

"The idea," said a spokesman, "is to get the fans in, let 'em see a game, and then let 'em go home." To make it ever more dull, the city fathers passed a law against making too much noise. Thus, the Metrodome is the only stadium in the major leagues where you can get arrested for cheering too loudly.

BRAVES FIELD
Boston • 1915–52

Braves Field was destined for shame.

The infield terrified fielders with its sinkholes. The outfield terrified batters with a playing surface so big, it could have been another country.

This ballpark's shameful history began before it was even a ballpark. The first job was to turn a golf course into a baseball field, and the workers hired to do that lived in fear of cave-ins. In 1914 a huge cave-in buried alive a dozen horses and mules along what later became the third-base line.

During one game a few years later, the shortstop area suddenly sank about eight inches, chasing a scared Rabbit Maranville to the dugout. He stayed there until the hole was filled.

For years the outfield was so big it became a power hitter's hell and a careless pitcher's heaven. With nearly 11 acres of playing surface, Braves Field had the largest outfield area in the majors.

The first time he saw the field, Ty Cobb squinted down the 402-foot foul lines and gazed at the out-of-sight center-field fence 550 feet away. Then he announced, "Nobody is ever going to hit one out of this place." Cobb was almost right. Not until 1925, ten years after the park was opened, did anyone knock the ball over the fence.

Between the endless outfield and the strong prevailing winds that blew in, low-scoring games were the rule. In 1928 Judge Emil Fuchs, owner of the Braves, decided to make it easier for his team to smack homers. The left-field fence was moved in to 353 feet, and the center-field fence was moved in to 387 feet. To the judge's dismay, the opposition hit twice as many four-baggers as the Braves. The next year Fuchs moved the fences back.

The ground-level scoreboard in left field also caused problems for the Braves. In 1916 New York Giants catcher Bill Rariden hit the only homer in the park all year. It happened when his drive bounced through an opening left in the manual scoreboard by a careless worker. Teammate Johnny Rawlings swatted a cheap home run the same way in 1922.

In 1946 the owners spent $500,000 to fix up the ballpark and improve goodwill among the fans. After the home opener, spectators in one section found their clothes dotted with green paint that had not had enough time to dry. The Braves ran ads in the daily newspapers to apologize and asked fans to send their cleaning bills to the club for payment. The team paid 5,000 claims—although more than 18,000 claims were filed, including some from as far away as California and Florida.

JARRY PARK
Montreal • 1969–76

Jarry Park was the world's only French-English outdoor insane asylum. You had to be nuts to play or attend a game there.

The bumpy infield and the rolling outfield at the Montreal Expos' first home drove more than a few fielders mad. After one pregame practice Pittsburgh's Bob Robertson snidely asked, "When do they let the cows out?"

In April, when the icy field began to thaw, runners had to contend with rubbery base paths. Sometimes the pitching mound and the area around home plate would actually sink a few inches. But it was fun watching the groundskeepers hurry to rebuild them.

To all the players, "Canadian Sunset" was not a lovely song, but a warning sign. During the first two weeks of June, the sunset blinded fielders at the start of night games. Thus, Jarry Park gave birth to "dusk doubles" and "twilight triples."

"Only here do I wear sunglasses for a night game," said Expo Ron Fairly in 1970. But the shades didn't always help the sure-handed first baseman. In the first inning of a game on June 13, 1970, Expos shortstop Bobby Wine fielded a ground ball and threw to Fairly. But the first baseman was blinded by the setting sun behind third base and never saw the throw. It sailed by his ear, and the runner ended up on second base. "The sun was so bad, I told Bobby Wine and (second baseman) Gary Sutherland they'd be better off to roll the ball to me," said Fairly.

The midday sun also bugged the players, especially in the early years. The huge lights were so clean that the sun's glare reflected off them and into the eyes of the fielders. "It may be the only place where someone lost a ball in the lights during a day game," mused Expos manager Gene Mauch.

The fans suffered right along with the players. The 30,000-seat single-deck structure offered no shelter at all from the snow, sleet, and cold rains of spring. And it offered no better protection when it came to the hot sun in the dog days of summer.

The ballpark even caused problems for people outside the stadium. There was a swimming pool just a few yards beyond the right-field fence. Besides watching the people in the pool, the lifeguards had to keep an eye out for home-run balls. They had to make sure the balls wouldn't conk some innocent swimmer on the head.

The Expos finally moved into Olympic Stadium— and shed no tears when they bid adieu to Parc Jarry.

PITIFUL PICKOFFS

The Most Boneheaded Pickoff Victims

Sometimes there's just no place to hide your shame no matter how hard you try. Nobody knows this better than the base runner who's just been picked off. He brushes the dirt off the front of his uniform. With his ears ringing from the jeers of the fans, he makes the long walk back to the dugout to face the sneers of his teammates. For "The Most Boneheaded Pickoff Victims," The Baseball Hall of SHAME inducts the following:

FRENCHY BORDAGARAY
Outfielder • Brooklyn, N.L. • Aug. 14, 1935

Frenchy Bordagaray had a talent for getting picked off second base, including once when he was standing on the bag!

It happened during a home game against the Chicago Cubs after the Dodger outfielder had reached

Frenchy Bordagaray got picked off second base—while he was still standing on the bag!

(George Brace Photo)

second base. Brooklyn manager Casey Stengel, who was coaching at first base, held up the game and went out to talk to Bordagaray.

"Now look here, Frenchy," said Stengel. "I want you to stand on second until the batter actually hits the ball. I mean stand right on the bag. Don't take a lead. Don't even move away from it six inches. Do you understand?"

"Why, certainly, Mr. Stengel," Frenchy replied.

Moments later pitcher Larry French whirled and fired a pickoff throw to second. Cubs shortstop Billy Jurges grabbed the ball and put the tag on Bordagaray for the out.

As the Frenchman passed Stengel on his way to the dugout, the angry manager hissed, "What were you doing out there? Why weren't you standing on the bag? How could they pick you off?"

"I haven't the slightest idea, boss," answered Bordagaray. "I did just like you told me. I didn't move from the base even three inches. I was just standing there tapping my foot on the bag, waiting for the next batter to bang one."

"I see," said Stengel, wiping the sweat from his heated brow. "In that case how did Jurges manage to put you out?"

Frenchy sighed and threw up his hands in defeat. "It beats me, boss. He must have put the tag on me between taps."

RON LeFLORE
Outfielder • Montreal, N.L. • July 28, 1980

Ron LeFlore knew that stealing bases takes concentration. But he learned the hard way that *staying* on base takes concentration, too.

In a game against Cincinnati at Olympic Stadium in Montreal, LeFlore stole second easily for his 62nd theft of the year. As he stood up and brushed himself off, he saw an interesting message on the electronic scoreboard. It was 115 years ago to the day that the first base ever stolen had been snatched by Ed Cuthbert.

Like many of the fans attending the game, LeFlore got really involved with this little bit of baseball trivia. Maybe too much so. While he was standing there *reading* about baseball, he forgot about *playing* it—and was promptly picked off second.

BARRY BONNELL   WILLIE UPSHAW
Outfielder   **First Baseman**

DAVE COLLINS
Outfielder
Toronto, A.L. • Aug. 24, 1983

In the most stunning display of sheer base-running bumbling in one inning, three Blue Jay runners reached first—and all three were picked off.

In the top of the tenth inning against the Baltimore Orioles, Toronto held a 4–3 lead with no outs and Barry Bonnell on first. Blue Jays manager Bobby Cox flashed the steal sign. After all, the Orioles had used up all their regular catchers and now had infielder Lenn Sakata behind the plate. The Blue Jays thought they could just stroll around the bases against the young catcher.

Eager to test Sakata's arm, Bonnell took his lead

off first. But Bonnell was a little bit too eager. Relief pitcher Tippy Martinez whipped the ball to first and caught Bonnell flat-footed for the first pickoff.

The next batter, Dave Collins, walked. He had the look of a man ready to take candy from a baby, but instead he got his own pocket picked. He strayed just far enough off first to become pickoff victim number two.

Now it was Willie Upshaw's turn to join the pickoff parade. After getting an infield hit he was all set to steal off Sakata when he got picked off like the others.

Incredibly, Martinez retired the side without getting a batter out.

As if that wasn't embarrassing enough for the Blue Jays, in the bottom of the tenth the Orioles tied the score. Then Sakata—the guy they were going to steal the game from—blasted a three-run homer to win the game for Baltimore, 7–4.

HERB WASHINGTON
Designated Runner • Oakland, A.L.
Oct. 13, 1974

Herb Washington showed beyond a shadow of a doubt that the idea of a designated runner—the brainchild of Oakland A's owner Charlie Finley—was way off base.

During the 1974 World Series, Washington proved what fans and players alike already knew. The designated runner had no business in baseball. In front of 60 million people watching the Series on TV, the Dodgers picked Washington off at first, snuffing out a ninth-inning rally.

Herb Washington, baseball's first designated runner, got picked off first in the 1974 World Series.

(AP/Wide World Photo)

Finley had picked Washington up from the college track circuit, where the speedster had run 100 meters in 10 seconds and 100 yards in 9.2. Washington was signed to play only as a pinch runner who would steal bases. Under his contract, he would never need to hold a bat or wear a glove.

Washington proudly donned his Oakland uniform for the 1974 season, but he never really got off the blocks the way Finley had planned. Washington appeared in 109 games in that season and part of the next, but he had only 30 steals in 48 attempts. St. Louis Cardinals base stealer Lou Brock could do that in a good six weeks.

The critics were all over Finley, but he was patient. He waited for the 1974 World Series to prove that his idea would work. At last Herb Washington could show the world how his dazzling speed and his daring baserunning would win one for the A's in a tight spot.

Washington's golden opportunity came in the ninth inning of the second game, with one out and the Dodgers leading 3–2. Pinch runner Washington, representing the tying run, edged away from first. Ever so carefully he widened his lead, his feet itching to spring toward second.

Like a cobra ready to strike, Washington stared at pitcher Mike Marshall. Marshall, like a mongoose ready to pounce, stared back. Washington stared. Marshall stared. Suddenly Marshall made his move. Washington didn't. The next sound Washington heard was the ball slapping into the glove of first baseman Steve Garvey. The next feeling he felt was that of getting tagged on the hand. The next thing he saw was umpire Doug Harvey's thumb in the air.

It was also one of the last things he saw in the bigs. Washington, the man who was born to run, was run out of baseball the following year.

The Most Disastrous
Farewell Performances

Everything comes to an end sooner or later, and that includes seasons, careers, franchises, and stadiums. Some go out in style. Others make their exit without any class at all, leaving behind a trail of shame that even a sanitation worker wouldn't touch. For "The Most Disastrous Farewell Performances," The Baseball Hall of SHAME inducts the following:

PITTSBURGH PIRATES'
WORLD CHAMPIONSHIP REIGN
Oct. 11, 1972

The world champion Pittsburgh Pirates were just three outs away from winning their second straight National League pennant. But with the title right in their hands, they threw it away on a historic wild pitch.

In the fifth and deciding game of the National League Championship Series in Cincinnati, the Pirates held a razor-thin 3–2 lead over the Reds. It was the bottom of the ninth inning, and ace reliever Dave Giusti was on the mound. Pittsburgh could already taste the champagne.

But on this day of all days Giusti didn't have his stuff. He gave up a dramatic game-tying homer and back-to-back singles. Then right-hander Bob Moose, normally a starting pitcher, relieved him. Moose retired the next batter on a long fly that advanced runner George Foster to third base, only 90 feet away from the pennant. Moose bore down and coaxed a pop-up. Now there were two outs. To send the game into extra innings, Moose absolutely had to retire hitter Hal McRae.

The count went to 1 and 1. Then Moose threw a hard slider down and away—but a little too down and a little too far away. The ball skipped into the dirt to the right of home plate and bounced over catcher Manny Sanguillen's head. The catcher hustled to retrieve the ball, but it was much too late. Foster had already raced across the plate with the pennant-winning run. There was nothing Sanguillen could do but fling the ball into center field. It was a final gesture of frustration over the embarrassing end to the Pirates' reign as world champs.

NEW YORK METS' LOSS
Sept. 11, 1974

For seven hours and four minutes the Mets battled the Cardinals in a 25-inning marathon that lasted so late even the night crawlers fell asleep.

Only 1,000 diehard fans from the original Shea Stadium crowd of 13,460 stayed until the final out at 3:13 A.M. It was one of the longest night games in major-league history.

So how did the Mets reward their fans' loyalty and staying power? New York blew the game on a play that would make a Little Leaguer wince.

The score was tied 3–3 in the top of the 25th inning when Met pitcher Hank Webb tried to pick Bake McBride off first base. The ball sailed past first baseman John Milner and bounded into right-field territory. McBride raced all the way to third. Then he decided there was no sense in stopping at that late hour and came charging home like an express train. He should have been derailed at the plate, because Milner's throw to catcher Ron Hodges arrived in plenty of time for the putout. But Hodges dropped the ball. McBride scored the winning run in the marathon game—thanks to two Mets errors on the same play.

WGRZ-TV'S TELECAST OF NOLAN RYAN'S NO-HITTER
Sept. 26, 1981

In the worst ending ever to a baseball telecast, Buffalo, New York, station WGRZ-TV pulled the plug on viewers watching a fifth no-hitter by Nolan Ryan.

It was a shameful reminder of the infamous *Heidi* football game on November 17, 1968. In that bungle the New York Jets were beating the Oakland Raiders 32–29 with 61 seconds left in the nationally televised game when NBC suddenly cut away. Why? To show its scheduled special movie, *Heidi*. Outraged viewers missed seeing the Raiders' dramatic two-touchdown comeback to win the thriller 43–32.

Thirteen years later TV viewers were once again left hanging in suspense. Only this time the viewers were those who turned to Buffalo's Channel 2 (then known as WRG-TV, an NBC affiliate).

The station showed the entire game between the Detroit Tigers and the Milwaukee Brewers on "NBC's Game of the Week." Then it picked up the network's backup game, in which Houston Astros hurler Nolan Ryan was no-hitting the Los Angeles Dodgers. At the end of eight innings, the Astros, battling for first place in the pennant race, were winning 5–0. Ryan had struck out 10 and walked three. Could he pitch another no-hitter?

Channel 2 viewers edged closer to their TV screens for the start of the all-important ninth inning. Then disaster struck. The station suddenly broke away from the exciting finish and switched to the program it had scheduled. The stunned and angry fans missed seeing Ryan mow down the last three Dodgers with a strikeout and two groundouts to make baseball history.

Just why did the station cut off the finish of Ryan's masterpiece, causing irate TV watchers to flood the station with calls of protest?

Channel 2 felt it had a duty to present *Life Aboard an Aircraft Carrier*—a naval training film!

FRED LINDSTROM'S CAREER
April 16, 1936

Future Hall of Famer Fred Lindstrom knew it was time to quit the game after the most embarrassing moment of his career.

Fred Lindstrom knew it was time to quit the game when he collided with a teammate while chasing a pop-up.

(AP/Wide World Photo)

When Lindstrom played for the New York Giants, he was recognized as the finest third baseman this side of Pie Trayner. Now he was playing left field for the Dodgers at the Polo Grounds against his old New York team. Brooklyn was winning 6–5 with two out in the bottom of the ninth. Giant runners Mel Ott and Burgess Whitehead were on first and second base respectively when Hank Leiber hit a high pop-up to short left field.

Lindstrom flipped down his sunglasses and raced in while shortstop Jimmy Jordan raced out. "I got it!" yelled Lindstrom. "I'll take it!" shouted Jordan. "Who's got it?" asked both.

As the ball plopped into Jordan's glove, the charging Lindstrom crashed into him, causing the ball to pop out and roll away. By the time it was retrieved, both Ott and Whitehead had raced home with the tying and winning runs for a lucky 7–6 Giant victory.

Afterward, in the losers' silent clubhouse, Lindstrom told his teammates, "I never thought it would happen to me. I'll tell you this, it's never going to happen again."

It was obvious that Lindstrom meant what he said that day. A month later the 13-year veteran quit the team and retired from baseball.

LOS ANGELES ANGELS' LOSS
Aug. 16, 1961

The Los Angeles Angels literally threw a game away on a final play that didn't even belong on a sandlot.

The visiting Angels were trying to hang on to a slim 2–1 lead in the bottom of the ninth inning against the

Washington Senators. In a last-ditch rally the Senators, with two outs, had runners Bud Zipfel and Marty Keough on first and second bases.

The next batter, Jim King, hit a routine grounder to Eddie Yost at third base. Yost effortlessly fielded the ball for what appeared to be the last out of the game. Angels manager Bill Rigney smiled and clapped his hands, ready to celebrate a victory.

To his dismay, Yost threw wildly past second baseman Rocky Bridges and blew the force-out. The ball sailed into right field as Keough scored the tying run. Rigney groaned in pain, but the worst was yet to come.

Right fielder Albie Pearson scooped up Yost's bad throw—and then fired one of his own, trying to nail Zipfel at third. Pearson pegged the ball over Yost's head and right between the legs of pitcher Jim Donahue, who was backing up the play. Zipfel then trotted home with the winning run.

Meanwhile, the ball bounded into the Angels' dugout and landed right on Rigney's lap. Angrily, he held the ball so tight that his knuckles turned white. Then he shoved it in his pocket, mumbling, "I'm going to keep this ball so it can't do any more damage."

THE ALL-TIME BASEBALL HALL OF SHAME AWARD

As great a game as baseball is, its reputation as America's pastime has been stained over the years by a myth. Baseball has overcome scandals, strikes, and lousy hot dogs but has yet to get rid of an ugly old blemish—the shame of shames. For this reason, The Baseball Hall of SHAME presents a special dishonor to the following:

A.G. SPALDING
Sporting Goods King

STEPHEN CLARK
Millionaire

KENESAW MOUNTAIN LANDIS
Commissioner of Baseball

The story that Abner Doubleday scratched out the design for a game on the Cooperstown village green in 1839 and thus invented baseball is a two-base falsehood.

Doubleday had nothing to do with the founding of baseball. And neither did Cooperstown. The tale was just part of a plot to sell more sporting equipment, boost tourism, and promote baseball.

At the turn of the century, sporting goods king A.G. Spalding decided to prove that baseball had been invented in America. It didn't matter that there was proof that it had evolved from the British games of rounders and cricket. Spalding figured that more Americans would buy his baseball equipment if they believed the game was born in the U.S.A.

In 1905 Spalding appointed a six-man commission to "discover" the game's true origin. But he wasn't about to let truth stand in the way of profit, so he didn't appoint any real investigators. Instead he stacked the commission with men who were out to prove—by hook or by crook—that baseball was 100 percent American.

On December 30, 1907, the Spalding Commission reported that baseball was invented by Abner Doubleday in 1839 in Cooperstown, New York. Their decision was based entirely on a letter from 73-year-old Abner Graves, who later ended up in a mental hospital for the criminally insane. Graves's letter claimed that 68 years earlier in Cooperstown he saw his boyhood pal Doubleday use a stick to draw plans in the dirt for a new game called baseball.

Balderdash! In 1839 Graves was only five years old, and Doubleday was nearly 20. Doubleday was a cadet at West Point, and no record exists of his leaving the academy in the summer of 1839. Besides, his family had moved out of Cooperstown in 1837.

On top of all that, Doubleday, who became a general and Civil War hero at Gettysburg, never even tried to take credit for inventing baseball. After retiring from the army in 1873, he published many articles and left 67 diaries. Not one of them mentioned baseball.

But Doubleday couldn't discredit the baseball lie. He had died in 1893—14 years before he was officially named the game's founder.

The Spalding Commission's report might have been forgotten had it not been for Cooperstown millionaire Stephen Clark. He decided the Doubleday tall tale might be a good way to sucker tourists into his out-of-the-way village. So in 1935 he started his scheme to establish a national baseball museum.

Clark had no trouble selling the idea to baseball's bigwigs. The Great Depression was hurting them at the turnstiles, and they were hungry for new ways to promote the game. They not only went along with the scam, they even planned a season-long celebration for baseball's "centennial" in 1939. Anything for a buck.

The National Baseball Hall of Fame and Museum was established in 1939 in Cooperstown, with honors bestowed upon Abner Doubleday. If the powers that be had been true to the game, the shrine would have been built in Hoboken, New Jersey. That was the *real* birthplace of modern baseball. And the honors would have gone to Alexander Cartwright, Jr.—the real originator of modern baseball.

Commissioner Kenesaw Mountain Landis knew the truth about the roots of the sport, but he ignored it. Before the "centennial" Landis received a letter from Cartwright's grandson, Bruce Cartwright. In it, Bruce documented the fact that it was his grandfather, Alexander Cartwright, Jr., and not Doubleday, who drew out the first baseball diamond and wrote the rules.

It's a matter of record that Alexander headed a rules committee in 1845 and established the foul lines, set the distance between the bases at 90 feet, and fixed the number of players on a side at nine.

The first game of baseball under the Cartwright rules was played on June 19, 1846. It took place on the old cricket grounds at Elysian Fields, a summer resort in Hoboken, New Jersey. The Knickerbocker Baseball Club (of which Cartwright was a charter member) lost to the New York Club 23–1 in a four-inning game.

Landis chose to close his eyes to these facts. Bruce Cartwright died a few weeks after writing to Landis, and his letter was filed away. Too much money and power were at stake for the lords of baseball to be bothered by the truth.

The only official recognition of Alexander Cartwright is a plaque at the Baseball Hall of Fame and Museum. It identifies him simply as "*a* father of modern baseball."

The schemers won: Spalding boosted sales of his baseball equipment; Cooperstown's coffers began filling up with tourists' money; and baseball promoted its phony roots.

Meanwhile, Abner Doubleday remains the unfounded founding father of baseball.

WHO ELSE BELONGS IN
THE BASEBALL HALL OF SHAME?

Do you have any nominations for The Baseball Hall of SHAME? Give us your picks for the most shameful, embarrassing, wacky, and boneheaded moments in baseball history. Here's your chance to pay a lighthearted tribute to the game we all love.

On separate sheets of paper, describe your nominations in detail. Those that are supported by the most facts, such as firsthand accounts, newspaper or magazine clippings, box scores, or photos, have the best chance of being inducted into The Baseball Hall of SHAME. Feel free to send as many nominations as you want. If you don't find a category listed in our Baseball Hall of SHAME books that fits your nomination, then make up your own. (All submitted material becomes the property of The Baseball Hall of SHAME and will not be returned.) Mail your nominations to:

The Baseball Hall of SHAME
P.O. Box 31867
Palm Beach Gardens, FL 33420

THE WINNING TEAM

The establishment of The Baseball Hall of SHAME is a lifelong dream come true for its two founders:

BRUCE NASH has felt the sting of baseball shame ever since he smashed a sure triple in a Pee Wee League game. He was almost thrown out at first because he was so slow afoot. He graduated to Little League but "played" his first and only season without ever swinging at a pitch. His most embarrassing moment on the field occurred in a sandlot game. A misjudged fly ball bounced off his head, allowing the winning run to score. As a die-hard Dodger fan in Brooklyn, Nash was so shocked by the team's surprise departure that he ended up rooting for the Yankees.

ALLAN ZULLO is an expert on losers. He rooted for the Chicago Cubs during their long cellar-dwelling years. Playing baseball throughout his childhood, he patterned himself after his Cub heroes. That explains why his longest hit in Pony League was a pop fly double that the first baseman lost in the sun. As a park league coach, Zullo achieved the distinction of piloting a team that did not hit a fair ball in either game of a doubleheader. Unaccustomed to the Cubs' extraordinary success in 1984 and 1989, Zullo has switched allegiance—to the Cleveland Indians.

Compiling and maintaining records is the important task of the Hall's curator, BERNIE WARD. His childhood baseball days followed a consistent and predictable pattern—consistently awful and predictably short. His teammates called him "the executioner." That's because he killed so many of his team's rallies by striking out or hitting into inning-ending double plays.